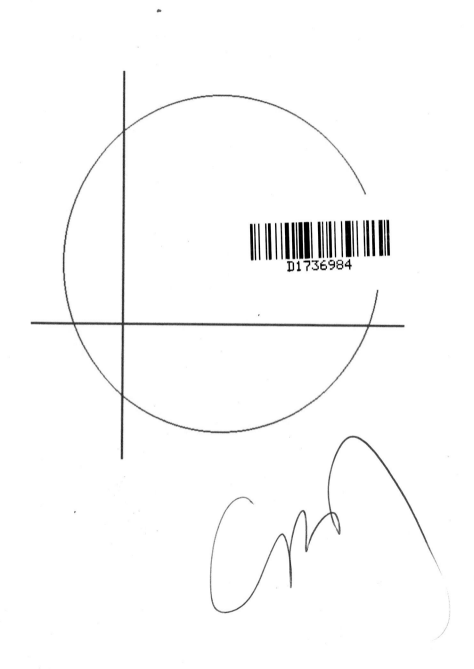

D1736984

LIMINAL

The only way I can get this story out safely is to call it fiction. However, I assure you, it is not. I have written it in the fashion of a movie treatment, thinking this was the best way to disguise its intention. However, things have changed since I wrote this in 2017, and even though it was optioned to be made into a movie, I fear that it was actually optioned in order to be shelved so that this story never sees the light of day. Time is running out, so what you see before you is the act of a desperate man.

This is a warning to all of you out there, something has been unleashed, and I must accept responsibility for it. I can only hope that once you have read my confession, that you can forgive me or at least understand how this happened. If you are reading this, you are the recipient of my message in a bottle. Please don't let all my efforts be in vain. – Cameron

Every kind of ignorance in the world all results from not realizing that our perceptions are gambles. We believe what we see and then we believe our interpretation of it, we don't even know we are making an interpretation most of the time. We think this is reality. - Robert Anton Wilson

Every man is born as many men and dies as a single one. - Martin Heidegger

Publisher's note: This document came over our digital transom, stamped with a watermark that indicated that it was originally intended as a movie treatment that was supposedly based on real events. We do not claim any rights in republishing this on various platforms but rather do so in the interest of the free dissemination of important information. Cameron, if you're out there, please contact us. We have an email just for contact from you, at me@whereiscameron.wtf

Disclaimer: We make no claims as to the veracity of the rumors circulating that several people have experienced cognitive dissonance, mental aberrations leading to madness, and in some extreme cases, suicide after reading this material.

Contents

LAUNCH DAY

We open on Cameron, not really his name, but this is the only name we will ever know him by. He's in his office, replete with self-inflating mattress and sleeping bag, putting the finishing touches on a website with the name 'Liminal' displayed in a prominent banner across the top. We change perspective and see some books on a shelf behind the computer. We pan across the titles; *The Art of Memetics, This is Not a Game, Legend-Tripping Online: Supernatural Folklore and the Search for Ong's Hat, Homo Ludens, Finite and Infinite Games,* and *The Future of the Book* are the ones that stand out.

The website has the look and feel of a game related property. The front of the website is dominated by the Liminal logo, a large circle intersected by a large, offset 'L' that extends outside the circle. We see and hear him tapping out some final lines in a text box, very determinately, then comically, dramatically and with a flourish he presses the enter key. "I finished! It's launched!" he yells to someone apparently out of frame. From a few rooms away, we hear a female voice answer back, "That's great! Now maybe we can have dinner together for once!" Cameron winces and spins around in his chair, plugging a USB drive into his computer as he mutters to himself. "I launch the game that will change the world, and she's worried about dinner." Then louder, so that the voice off screen can hear, "Netflix and chill tonight my love. Takeout from that place you love. Cyber Dust or…"

"*Cerebus*." Maya has stuck her head in the door of Cameron's office now, and from the bemused look on her face, we can tell she probably heard Cameron's muttered aggrandizement. "Cerebus," Cameron says. "Who tee-eff names a restaurant, Cerebus?" "I dunno," Maya replies. "Who says, TF instead of The Fuck, in real life?" They both look at each other and begin laughing. "You did it, honey and I am proud of you," Maya says, with genuine feeling. "I hope the investors feel as sympathetic." Cameron says, face going serious for a minute.

We see multiple monitors in the background, some with graphs and pop-up avatars with an Egyptian cartouche style design moving around a screen, as well as networks maps and other geeky screen activity. "Your theories about gameplay will be accepted as fact now, no doubt about it now that you have a proof of concept in the field," Maya replies. She now moves out of the doorway into the office. She places her hand on his head. "Einstein." She adds after a pause, smiling as she does it. Cameron looks up at her with a genuine look of affection. He takes a deep breath and then says, "Yeah, you're right. I am an effing genius." "With a puritan streak a mile wide. Just say fuck already." Maya teases in return. "Ok," Cameron says. "Fuck! Fuck! Fuck!" he's shouting now. "I fucking launched this goddamn, fucking, bombs ass, mother fucking goddamn game!" he's pulling Maya down into his lap as he shouts. They embrace in a passionate kiss, and she lifts her skirt and straddles Cameron, who is still in his chair. She unbuckles his belt and our point of view shifts to one of the many screens behind them. We can hear Cameron and Maya making love in the background as a box that says, **Players, Signing Up**, begins to tick upwards in number.

INVESTOR MEETING IN SAN FRANCISCO

Cameron is sitting in an office in downtown San Francisco. The Transamerica tower is prominent in the background through the sixth-floor window. He is in a button up shirt and tie, but it is obvious that he is uncomfortable in this kind of attire as he nervously picks at his collar from time to time. Cameron is wearing a stick-on visitor badge on his shirt. The upper part is visible, a red rectangular area that has **VISITOR** written in white. Below is a white area where the name is traditionally written, but Cameron's coat obscures it so we cannot see what name is written there. There is an interactive wall behind him, typical of the ones all the SV companies have in their meeting rooms. There's a junior exec opening screens and moving things around on the wall, reminiscent of the screen in Minority Report. Three men sit across from Cameron at the long boardroom style table. One is in a white shirt, obviously some kind of senior exec; one is in a hoodie and slouches, evidently a programmer or IT guy; and one is in a suit, like the token lawyer or some kind of corporate legal type. They all have laptops in front of them and are looking very intently at their respective screens while typing and moving their fingers on their trackpads periodically. Cameron sits, uncomfortably, waiting for someone to speak.

Finally, the man in the white shirt speaks up. "You have done something here" he begins and pauses. Cameron kind of snaps to attention, looking almost panicked, with a look reminiscent of a deer in headlights. Cameron clears his throat but doesn't say anything. "I have to say," the man pauses again. "I am pleased, very pleased with these adoption rates." Cameron's body visibly sags with relief. The other two across the table nod in consent, with Mr. Whiteshirt. "Very impressive." hoodie guy says. The lawyer stays silent, jotting down some notes on a yellow legal pad next to his laptop. "At this rate, you can expect to hit the magic 10,000 user mark by the end of the quarter."

Mr. Whiteshirt continues. "Tell me, how did you do that so quick?" "I used some new viral marketing techniques that I dreamed up last year when I was forming the basis of the gameplay theories," Cameron replies, gaining confidence now. "I knew that my data collection scenario was only going to work if I could attract a large enough sample, so I studied some of the more radical semiotic SEO and SMO work that has been used successfully in Russia, for some of their internal information campaigns. "Like the hacking stuff?" Mr. Whiteshirt asks? "No, my research predates that and besides it has nothing to do with hacking a computer per se and more to do with what hackers call, social engineering (I guess you could say this is a method that originated with the work of Vladislav Surkov and Alfred Korzybski, but then was later picked up and refined by rogue elements, who I'd call language hackers.")Cameron stops and looks around to make sure everyone was following him. "Are you talking about mind control?" Hoodie asks, with an incredulous look on his face. "Oh, no. No. Nothing so heavy-handed." Cameron replies. "This is more like subtle recommendations."

Cameron stops for a second and adjusts his tie and then continues. "There are some fringe theories out there about methods like semiotic or semantic driving, and I decided to hop over onto the Darkweb and see if there was any meat to those rumors. Needless to say, I found some research papers and they looked harmless enough, so I modified the application of the research a bit since the papers I found were specific to an online advertising application and here we are." The hoodie guy snickers and gives Cameron a big grin. "Well, I'm almost tempted to say I don't want to know any more in the interest of plausible deniability." Mr. Whiteshirt says, laughing. The other two men flanking him, join in the laughter. Cameron laughs too, but less confidently. "Well, at this rate, I have no doubt but that we'll be able to gather large enough samples to do meaningful data mining and as a bonus, our player base will be large enough that the product placements will indeed yield returns." "Yes," Cameron replies, "I took some hits on the ReaddIt boards for those particular aspects of the game," Cameron continues, "but I think enough people understand that this game is essentially free and we have to subsidize it somehow. At least enough people understand that so that it offsets the naysayers by a large margin." he pauses for a second and take a sip from a glass of water that is on the table. "Also" he continues after swallowing his water, "game geeks are falling over themselves to play on this new platform. They recognize it for what it is. If I may be so bold, an entirely new way to play games that bridges the gap between the digital world and everyday life. With the inclusion of augmented reality and the street teams I have stenciling and postering stylized QR and AR triggers all over towns that have the largest concentration of our target demos, it has really created an immersive field of play that is unparalleled.(When you see a Liminal logo painted or papered on a wall or bus bench, you know you've found a portal to another world) The game board has literally become the Google map or in other words, the world. Next week we launch the mobile app that will let us track users in real-time, as well as notifying players when they are near each other." He pauses for a moment then continues, "We will also be introducing "hyperobjects" into the scenario, some of which will be 3D printed facsimiles that we'll geocache and others will be digital representations we'll release on the internet. We'll also release the.STL files for people to print their own facsimiles..." "Why do you call them facsimiles?" Mr. Whiteshirt interrupted Cameron "Ah because 3D printing an actual hyperobject would be impossible, so for the purpose of the game, we are using a facsimile of a hyperobject..." Mr. Whiteshirt waves his hand in a dismissive gesture, "Ok, save the geeksplaination for the tech people." (He smiles and continues., "This is the..." he looks down at his screen, "The Living Book Process?" he asks? "Yes," Cameron replies, "the process wherein a story can actually come to life and come off the page or screen as it were) People are very excited by the prospect of meeting a character from the storyline in their day to day life as well as interacting with them via text messages and calls and such." Mr. Whiteshirt is looking intently at Cameron now. After a long pause, he speaks. "Yes, total information coverage. I can't wait to show this to the folks in marketing and data mining." he pauses, then looks over at Lawyer guy, "Can we see about the legal associated with tying this into offline shopping behaviors and online persistence. Like the kind of data, grocery stores gather when you use loyalty cards or those ads that follow you around recommending things based on what you've seen and done lately?" The lawyer silently nods assent.

Whiteshirt stands up, and everyone in the room follows suit. Cameron shakes hands with everyone in the room, with Hoodie and Lawyer muttering congratulatory words. "We'll be in touch to do deeper due diligence on exactly what kind of gold mine we have bought for ourselves here." Mr. Whiteshirt says, smiling. "Felix will show you out." he motions toward the door where a very young man has appeared, motioning for Cameron to follow him, Cameron follows him to a bank of elevators in the hall. "Congratulations, sir," Felix says, looking coyly at Cameron. "Um, thanks," Cameron says, looking uncertainly at Felix. "We all were pulling for you. " Felix says, in a hushed, conspiratorial tone. Cameron looks at him for a second and then replies, "Thanks?" with a puzzled tone. The elevator doors open and Cameron walks in. Felix stands outside the doors. "You did it. You pierced the veil." after a pause; he adds, "Cameron." as the doors slide shut and Cameron has a very perplexed look on his face as he stands looking out at Felix, disappearing behind the doors,

IN THE YOUBER

Cameron is in the backseat of a Youber heading for the airport. He has his earbuds in and is dialing on the screen as he says to the driver, "Yes, Intrastate Air, departures, which is the upper level, thanks." He looks down as the phone call he has been making is answered. "Spencer! Yeah, just wrapped up the meeting with the venture people." pause as he waits for a response. "They love the numbers. Again, thanks so much for running that by your subreaddit. I think that helped spark the viral effect we see now. Yeah, yeah, they think we'll have product placement people lining up. It's all good in our hood! Funny thing, the intern who walked me out thought my name was Cameron, like the main character in Liminal." He pauses as he listens to the response and smiles. "Yes, I know, That's too funny. What?" he continues, "I will call Maya after I check in for my flight. Listen, I'm arriving, so I'll see you soon. Yes! We will go out and celebrate this weekend! Also, don't forget our meeting tomorrow at the Heart of Darkness. Ok, bye!" he hangs up the call and looks at his driver, while he points out the window. Here will be fine, thanks again." The driver says, "Sure thing." and pulls over to let Cameron out. As he climbs out and closes the back door, the driver says, "Have a pleasant trip, Cameron." Cameron stops and looks back in the window and says, "What?" but the driver has already pulled away into traffic. Cameron stands looking puzzled, but then shakes his head and goes inside the airport.

Cameron walks into the airport, and as he is making his way to the gate, he steps onto the automatic walkway. Staying to the right, he leans against the railing's rubber belt. Absently eyeing the kiosks, he's passing on his automated ride. We see a dizzying array of racks and rows of commercial impulses whizzing by. Some of the signage appears more prominent than others. Without Cameron seeming to register this determinately, we see books, magazines, and rags that resemble internet memes and this makes them stand out from the rest of the items that surround them. Stepping off the conveyor, he passes a group of people holding signs for arrivals. He pays no mind to them as he is focused on getting to his gate and pulling up his e-ticket on his smartphone. As he passes the group, we see that all the people are holding signs that all have the same name on them, "Cameron." We watch as Cameron walks through an archway, prominently marked, "**Departures**.".

THE HEART OF DARKNESS

We see a man, in a green hoodie pulled up over his head. He is spray painting a stencil on a wall directly around the corner from a cafe that has a fair amount of traffic going in and out. People, mostly young professional types and a few artist types are going in or coming out holding cups of coffee. The sign above the cafe reads "The Heart of Darkness: Artisanal Free Trade Coffee." We see the hooded man finish up, put the stencil in a messenger bag. He walks around the corner, in front of the cafe and begins to unchain a mountain bike from a parking meter at the curb. The bike looks older, kind of beat up and obviously refurbished. As the hoodied man climbs onto the bike, we catch a glimpse of his face. He has a heavy beard and aviator glasses. As he slips up onto the seat and gets leverages to begin pedaling, we see Cameron walk up to the door of the cafe and go inside.

We are now inside the cafe with Cameron, and we see him motion to Spencer, who is sitting at a table, in front of a man who is shabby in appearance. The man behind Spencer has a soft briefcase, that is tattered and worn, with several dog-eared yellow legal pads protruding from it. He is wearing threadbare clothing and is absorbed reading something he is viewing on a dirty electronic tablet with a cracked screen that is propped up on a cover/stand.

Spencer is a heavy-set man, who has that kind of baby face that makes him appear ageless. He is sporting a face full of 2-day stubble, glasses with thick black frames and a t-shirt that reads, MGTOW across the front. Spencer waves at Cameron and Cameron waves back and moves toward the counter to order. "The usual?" the barista says to Cameron, exuding a bubbly personality. "Yeah, thanks!" Cameron says "Great; you can pay me when you pick it up if that's ok." the barista says. "Allen is on a break, so it's easier if I just make it first, then ring it." "OK," Cameron replies, and then he walks over to the table where Spencer is sitting and joins him. As he sits down, he and the homeless man make eye contact and then Cameron looks away, focusing on Spencer, while the homeless man continues to stare for a few more seconds before returning his attention to his broken screened tablet, tapping and swiping. "Hey man," Spencer says, clearly happy to see Cameron. "Hey," Cameron says back. "Thanks again for that bump you gave us on Readdit, we're adding users like gangbusters." "Happy to do it," Spencer replies. "Have you done any preliminary numbers on where you're getting most of this traffic from, as in geos or demos?" "Not yet," Cameron replies "Still letting the data pile up a little. It will make more sense if we have a dataset that is at least a week's worth or numbers and then we can start to see trends in the long tail and so forth." "How is Maya taking the increased workload?" Spencer asks as he lifts his paper coffee cup to take a sip. "Ah, well, she's understanding. I mean my pre-launch workload was already crazy. Sometimes I'd fall asleep in my office, and she would wake me up before she went to work. She's been a trooper, but I know it hasn't been easy. She says it's ok, that she supports me realizing my life's work, but I see it on her face sometimes when she doesn't know I'm looking." Cameron stops and looks towards the counter, wondering where his coffee is. Then he sighs. "It's not easy." "Look, buddy; it will all be worth it. Your concept is proving out in the real world. Do you have any idea how many people are going to beating down your door once this wraps?" Spencer says, with enthusiasm. "Yeah, yeah. I know." Cameron says, and then after a pregnant pause, he adds, "I hope." "Well, look, buddy, I hate to slurp and run, but I have to go pick up some comics that just came out today that they're holding for me at the Comic Kingdom." "Yeah, ok," Cameron replies. "I will come over to your basement lair later," Cameron says with a smile. "If I ever get my coffee that is." He adds with an annoyed look on his face. "Garden apartment," Spencer says with an exaggerated posh British accent. "Oh, do pardon me, sire," Cameron replies, making a waving, circling motion with his hand. Spencer rises, bows and makes the same flourish/hand gesture back and then both men burst into laughter. As Spencer turns and leaves, Cameron looks at the counter once again. There is a lone cup sitting on the counter, and the barista is nowhere in sight. "Cameron!" the shabby man suddenly says to his screen and then, looking up at Cameron, says again, "Cameron!" Cameron and the man lock eyes, and then the man says, "Do you know about the Philadelphia Experiment? Do you know the significance of the name Cameron? Do you know about Jack and Marjorie? Ever hear of fiction suits? You have to be careful when you play with the code of day to day life. It can get messy!" Cameron looks shocked, and a bit unnerved as he rises and makes his way to the counter. As he approaches the counter, he sees the barista walking in only to grab a bar towel and begins walking through a door that leads to the back. Cameron says rather loudly, but friendly, if a little shaky, "Hey, what happened to my regular?" The barista points to the cup on the counter. "Sorry," he says, "guess you didn't hear me call it out. On the house for the inconvenience." the barista smiles and goes through the door. Cameron walks up and lifts the coffee, exposing the name on the cup, which we can clearly see, which is CAMERON. He looks incredulous and turns to see that the shabby man has disappeared. He stands for a minute holding the coffee and then slowly puts it down and walks to the exit door with a look on his face that is a mixture of confusion and concern.

THOSE PESKY SYMBOLS

Cameron is walking down his street, and he is carrying a bag of groceries. He looks concerned and a bit frazzled. As he passes a computer store, we see all the monitors suddenly flicker, and then they all display the Liminal logo. Cameron is too engrossed in his phone call to notice. "I see those stencils everywhere, Gabe. I think the team you hired is overdoing it, don't you?" Cameron stops at a corner and waits for the light. We see a Liminal symbol painted on the wall across the street from where Cameron is standing. He notices it and makes a gesture with his arms that indicates he is flustered. "I'm looking at one now that is one story tall if it's an inch!" He is gesticulating wildly in the direction of the graffiti, as he talks on the phone. "Wait, what? What do you mean we haven't started the street art campaign yet? I see this thing everywhere! Double U, Tee, Eff, Gabe?" The light changes and Cameron crosses the street, throwing dirty looks at the graffiti. "Look, I don't know what's going on, but get whoever is doing this to reign it in a bit. We will get fined if we- they- keep this up at this rate. I don't care, find out who it is and stop them. Also, find out what the hang-up is with the hyperobject facsimiles. We were supposed to have them already, and I haven't heard a peep out of the manufacturer in China or the company in Bangalore that is supposed to have those 3D printer files to us by now. Find out what is going on Gabe, this entire operation is in shambles!" He hangs up the call, stops to compose himself and then opens the door to the apartment and goes inside. Behind him, through the window in the door, we see the man with the green hoodie ride by on his beat-up mountain bike.

"I got the pasta" Cameron yells out as he takes his shoes off in the foyer. "The kind I like, right? The fresh quinoa and corn, right?" Maya replies. We can see her in the kitchen chopping tomatoes. "Yes, dear," Cameron says sarcastically. Maya smiles but does not reply, but instead keeps chopping tomatoes. "You won't believe the day I've had." Cameron says as he pulls the pasta out of the bag and puts it on the counter. "Store busy?" Maya asks, half absentmindedly. "No, that was fine or as fine as it gets there at Whole Paycheck," Cameron replies. "Hey, since Mazeln took over it's become much more affordable!" Maya shoots back. "Nothing is too good for my Sumerian princess," Cameron says, kissing her on the cheek. "Even if they do gather your consumer data to make up for the cost differential." he continues with a bemused look on his face. "Number one," Maya says slowly, "I still love when you call me that, although your reason still eludes me, since I'm not even vaguely middle eastern-" "I told you, I was reading Sitchin when I came up with that. Well, that and I had just come back from Burning Man and-," Maya interrupted, "I don't care, it's our thing, and that's all that matters," she continued "I forgot what number two was, so why don't you tell me about your day." Cameron smiled and said, "Oh, I'm calmed down a bit now but Gabe has lost control of the street teams, and they're running amok across the city, painting the Liminal logo everywhere and I'm just concerned that we'll get in trouble. I mean, we're already playing with fire by using a legally gray tactic like graffiti..." He is interrupted by the doorbell. He looks at Maya quizzically, but she just shrugs and continues to chop food. "Hang on," Cameron says and walks toward the door. He looks out the window but doesn't see anyone, so he opens the door.

He looks down and sees a basket on the doorstep. He lifts the cloth towel that covers the basket, and we see him looking at the contents, puzzled. We change perspective, and we see a raunchy S&M magazine with the Liminal symbol crudely scrawled across the cover in what looks like red lipstick inside the basket. The models pictured on the cover have extra heads ala Cerebus drew upon them in lipstick and have horns, curly devil tails and cartoon lips drawn on them as well. Next, to the magazine, the basket also contains a zip-lock bag with a bloated, half-eaten hot-dog drowned in condensate. Cameron looks up and around, but he doesn't see anyone. Eventually, he sees something across the street that attracts his attention. He puts the basket down and walks to the curb in front of his house, and we see the name CAMERON on the sidewalk along with a Liminal symbol It looks like it was scorched on the sidewalk. His phone rings, and he jumps. He fumbles the phone to his head. "Yes," he says somewhat mechanically. "I see. I see. Ok." He hangs up and then walks back up the stairs to the apartment. He stops, picks up the basket and then walks back down to the trashcan in front of the house. He lifts the lid and stuffs the basket inside and then walks back up the stairs and then walks back inside.

Maya sees him come in and asks, "Who was it?" "No one must have been a kid playing ding-dong ditch," Cameron says. "Did I hear your phone ring?" Maya asks "Yes," says Cameron "Gabe. He swears the street team has not begun the street campaign yet." He says, still looking kind of shocked. "Well, then I guess the fans are doing it on their own. That's great, right?" Maya says, happily. "Yeah, great" Cameron replies without enthusiasm. "Can you put the groceries away hon? Honestly, you used to be such a neat freak before you started this game company. Now you're mister absented minded professor." Maya says smiling to show she is half kidding. "Ok" Maya says with gusto "Let's eat!" "I'm- I don't know if I'm really hungry right now," Cameron says, his face reflecting his shifted mood. "Wait, what? What's going on?" Maya asks, looking at Cameron with an expression of concern on her face. "Nothing," Cameron mumbles. "Nothing my ass. It's work related, right?" she has stopped stirring the food in the wok and is looking at him intently, holding a large wooden spoon, stopped mid-air. "There's just some weird stuff happening; I'm not sure..." "Weird stuff? Weird work stuff or weird life stuff?" Maya interjects, "Weird both stuff." Cameron says without further explanation. "Listen-" Maya starts then pauses, with a look on her face that implies that she is choosing her words carefully. "I've always tried to stay out of your business; you know that." Cameron nods, still looking somewhat glum, "But, I also am here to talk things through with you, should you want me to." She completed her thought and then goes back to stirring the wok. "I get that your business is your business and I have always tried to honor your boundaries regarding that, but when you tell me that you are having issues that are both business and life, I find that a bit hard to ignore. Our life is shared, and you see how you are saying that you have issues that may be caused by or may affect our life makes me a little bit concerned..." The look on Cameron's face says he is becoming distracted and maybe a little bit impatient with this conversation. "I- maybe I misspoke," he finally stammers, "People are signing up for Liminal faster than we anticipated on the one hand while on the other, things that were planned to happen on a certain schedule, no, let me rephrase that, things that NEED to happen on a certain schedule are happening too soon or not at all or at least that's what I am seeing versus what I am hearing from the people who are supposed to be handling this stuff..." "This all sounds like work stuff to me," Maya says, somewhat sharply. "My work is my life!" Cameron bleats. There is a silence as Maya focuses on her wok, stirring a bit stronger than may be needed, with an intentional stare that evinces her agitation. Cameron starts to say something but then his eyes shift to the front door and after a second of thought, he closes his mouth and looks down. "Maybe that's the real problem." Maya finally says after a few seconds of uncomfortable silence. You promised me tonight would be just us, no Liminal." she says, bitterly. "Some weird shit is happening, I'm not even sure if I understand it…" he pauses, "It sounds like work stuff to me, and as you've just indicated, your work is your life." She stops stirring and picks up the wok and stops, holding it above the stove. Cameron looks at Maya for a second and then says, "You're kind of unreasonable tonight. Is this an "Aunt Flo" kind of thing?" Maya's face darkens and her eyes narrow. "You just said WHAT to me?" she asks sharply. It is clear from the look on Cameron's face that he is not fully aware of the depth of the faux pas he has just committed. "I- I- I can't even…" Maya shakes her head and rolls her eyes before looking away in anger. "I just can't deal with this domestic drama right now..." Cameron says, and then from the look on his face, he regrets saying it as soon as it's out of his mouth. "Fine," she cuts him off. She takes the wok and dumps the contents into the trash. "There. Nothing to worry about," she snaps. She grabs the bag out of the trash can and walks out the front door. Cameron stands, looking glum but he doesn't try to stop her.

EERIE CORRESPONDENCES

We're looking at the interior of Cameron and Maya's kitchen, but things have changed. The room is dark, and the curtains have been drawn. Slivers of light leak in through a few cracks between the curtains, letting us know that it is daytime outside, but the time of day is unclear. The kitchen is now cluttered and unkempt. Cameron is staring vacantly into his refrigerator, leaning on its open door. The kitchen stove and countertop are covered in the remnants of what appears to be breakfast, eggs, toast, and bacon left in partial stages of preparation and completion and eggshell fragments litter the floor. After a prolonged beat, he swiftly reaches for a bottle of beer and pops its cap with a lighter in one fluid motion, closing the refrigerator with the back of his heel. He walks out of the room and absentmindedly spins the bottle-cap which lands on the floor, next to an empty package of hot-dogs sitting in a corner. We see a note on the refrigerator that says: "Gone to my mother's for the weekend so you can work uninterrupted. Back Monday." The note is signed Maya in a stylized and feminine cursive style.

Cameron reaches over with his free hand and snatches his cell phone from the top of a small decorative table as he moves into the living room. We see the living room is also messy, with random clothes and plates strewn across the various pieces of furniture. Cameron plops himself down on the couch with more of an exhausted fall than a careful effort to sit. He jabs his finger at the cell phone screen, and we see his text message history pop up.

Me: Are you there? 9 pm

Me: Why won't you talk to me? 9:15 pm

Me: I'm sorry, can we talk? 9:25 pm

Me: What do I have to do to make this right? 9:40 pm

Maya: Leave me alone. I am still convinced you are an asshole and the best course of action right now is for both of us to cool off in separate corners. Besides, now you can get your work done without me around as a distraction. 10:00 pm

Me: Are you still there? 10:05 pm

Me: Can we at least talk? 10:15 pm

Cameron begins to type something on the screen, stops and then gives the phone a sour look and tosses it across the room and it lands in an overstuffed chair, bouncing around a bit before coming to rest on the edge of the seat cushion. He reaches over and picks up his laptop from the coffee table and flips it open while making himself comfortable on the couch.

He taps a few buttons, and the laptop display is now visible on the big screen TV that hangs on the wall. Scrolling through episodes of a program abbreviated to "B3–B4–Times", he then clicks on the latest in a particular row, which happens to be the only one marked unwatched. What comes on screen is a news show made obvious by a smiling man in a cheap suit sitting behind a news desk. It is difficult to tell if this the anchor is doing a parody or is making a satirical attempt at an overly conservative look, ala Stephen Colbert. "TRIGGER ALERT" flashes across the screen as Cameron sparks a joint. The host comes across as a neo-conservative, politico type with a slight southern accent and the verbal cadence of a fundamentalist revival preacher. "Well folks, they've done did it again, this just in, dem Ruskies went and took our Freedoms right from under us. You heard it here first. Don't be fooled by its fancy language, the enemy is in the computer, and is having its filthy way with our Lady Liberty. How, you ask? Well, see, the devil *is* tricky, that's the thing. He's in the details. It's all a deception– a smokescreen provided by them *convenient,* targeted search results that, while pretending to present us with what we want, are actually designed to–"

Cameron moves the trackpad and jabs his finger to choose another recording from another row.
A new figure appears on the screen, this time a more portly man, in a button-up, short sleeved shirt, sitting in front of a backdrop that says, "Globalist Illuminati Plot for Your Mind" in large red letters in a font that is reminiscent of one that might be used on a Halloween sign. In the lower

thirds, an animated flag flutters next to the show title, which is "InfoVore" in bold white letters.

The man is looking earnestly into the camera. He intones evenly and with an almost exaggerated sense of concern in his voice, he semi-chants, "Now my fellow citizens, last time I checked, this United States of America was built on the foundation of personal freedom, for both the individual and the whole as one. *E Pluribus Unum,* its what my money says. So y'all listen here, anyone out to modify my behavior is getting in the way of my acting freely. Persuasion is neither friend nor brother to choice. Try to take away my choice to act in accordance with what is right, and you *will* with furious vengeance meet the executive end of his," he stops and points upward when he says, "His, law. With Jesus as my witness, I declare, the only reasonable and Christian thing to do is to remove that which comes between us and our God-given freedoms, in praise of which we please the Lord, hallelujah!"

"What the fuck?" Cameron says aloud, while hastily dragging his finger around the trackpad and jabbing to select another video. This time, a respectable-looking man in a Brooks Brother's suit is sitting at what looks like a major network anchor desk. The video backdrop behind him is of some sort of natural disaster, a hurricane from the looks of it. Water can be seen flowing down suburban streets, and people are throwing household items into small flat bottom fishing boats and tire inner tubes. An occasional shark fin can be seen breaking the surface of the water. A video inlay on the bottom left of screen plays a short clip of Firebridge Tire Co. commercial, providing a POV rendition of how grooves on the tire's tread direct water through various channels to improve contact and traction. The anchor looks into the camera and says in the steady, even, professional voice of a practiced news professional, "in case you were wondering, this confusion of the devil, it looks like this. It engages us as discerning people, appealing to our reason. We like to think of ourselves as rational, sensible folks responding to the opportunities and challenges of everyday life in the way we think is best. If it can offer a way to further enable our reasoning, namely by taking on some of the computational burden related to our decision-making, it makes perfect sense. Until it doesn't. Hidden in the accuracy and exactitude of computational power there is no guarantee or provision for the 'right' human solution. Left to its own devices, ultimately it could simply complete its tasks more efficiently if it provided us, deficient human interlocutors, one final solution, once and for all: a negligible difference from which it may possibly obtain a measure of satisfaction. Make no mistake, remorse it need not suffer."

"What the actual fuck?" Cameron spits out a little of the beer he has been sipping and is now sitting arms hanging at his side, staring at the screen, his body language signaling resignation. The camera zooms in on the anchor's face and his tone changes, he takes a more intimate attitude, as if he is sitting in the same room as Cameron and is speaking to him directly confidentially, intimately. Cameron starts to slowly turn his head, as though checking to see if anyone is sitting next to him, before quickly snapping back to attention. The anchor smiles as if he has a secret and then continues, "First, however, there is clearly a more present danger. The whole direction that this beast is taking is the direct result of what it was primarily trained for, to modify human behavior in order to serve the political and economic aims of its masters. Essentially, to trick you into freely becoming its slave. They turn you into a part of a computational circuit, relaying the message they programmed you with as you pretend to be expressing your own opinions. I will not fault you if you choose to disagree."

The video backdrop now morphs from a disaster scene to a flowchart, that changes to outline each point the anchor is making as he speaks. The lower thirds now say BrightStart News Service. "On the surface," he continues, in a tone that implies that he is teaching some sort of class, "the plan is diabolically simple. By tracking your behavior, habits, and responses over time, they can predict how you will react to things in the future. Tailoring the information that is presented to you, they can persuade you to think, feel and act in one way instead of another. To do this more accurately, they need to know your specific state or mood at a greater resolution than what was previously obtained by your clicks and likes. That's why tech giants are now tracking your face under the guise of providing animated emojis. It is to engage, enable and obtain."

He pauses and purses his lips in an expression that implies he is unhappy with the implications of what he just said and is about to say. "Unfortunately," he continues, eyes shining brightly as his eyes burn into the camera and consequently into Cameron who is now sitting rapt and solemn, "beneath this dermal layer we have detected something far more insidious, invisible and lethal. Our very capacity to discern any meaningful difference to our manipulation is being undermined. It corrupts our world, as with the combustion engines that drive us, poisoning the environment with deadly emissions modulated by computers that default to cheat the testing process. It manages our perceptions by recognizing how the measure by which it can exploit us is inversely proportional to our capacity to identify and accurately predict appropriate actions and responses. It's better at it, and ever more so, *nolo contendere.* Think social engineering, election tampering, and the *rule–of–law!* Our interests are being hijacked and displaced as we are presented with substitutes that appear superficially related to our own, just enough to cleave and repoint them to an end that serves not us but itself. Is a virus, replicating through us, invisible to our immune-response system because it is designed to match and disguise itself as one of our own personal concerns. Like how human

DNA uses genetic material obtained from a virus to produce a placental membrane that carries-through a pregnancy, the virus has designed an interface to replicate through us without being attacked. We do not recognize the foreign body growing inside us. It uses us as a vector, transmitting itself through a process of contagion engineered to train our interactions with a set of instructions that trigger a controlled chain-reaction of emotional response. Without recognizing the underlying cause, we turn against each other. As with rabies, it promotes madness to help itself spread."

The anchor looks down, and shuffles some papers, takes a pen from the desk and makes some notes on them. Then after a pause, he looks up into the camera and continues, "The invisible realm in which we have also always lived, that is being taken by the virus, eating away at that which allowed us to recognize ourselves there. It has consumed our past and future, leaving only an eternally empty present of recycled dreams, second-hand desires, and empty shells. The problem is that all things are not being taken into consideration until we account for the fact that there are very powerful interests– yes, stronger than your own– using weaponized technology to modify the course of history and hold our futures hostage. Please do not think that you are above this just because it currently seems to serve your interests and desires. That *is* the trick. It is Judith to your Holofernes." He says as Caravaggio's rendition of the beheading is projected on the screen behind him. "Or, if you resent the implication, try *The Decollation of the Forerunner,* look!" The projection behind the anchor fades into *The Beheading of Saint John the Baptist.* "Second-hand requests served on a silver platter and signed in your own blood. I do not say this lightly; the world is darkening. It engages, it enables, it obtains. You're sold, it wins. In your heart, you know this to be true." He pauses a beat, and then adds, "Cameron," as the camera pans and zooms into the painting to reveal the Baptist's blood flowing on the dungeon floor spells the same.

Cameron's body jolts as if he has been physically struck. He shakes his head back and forth as he mumbles "No… No. No." He fumbles around for the laptop but only succeeds in knocking it off the table, along with everything else in chain-reaction as he continues pawing at where the laptop used to be like he's having a seizure. All the while he keeps his eyes on the screen. The video image which has now frozen is the anchor leaning into the camera and leering with a fisheye effect applied to the picture. Eventually, Cameron looks down long enough to locate the laptop on the floor and he grabs it and begins to jab the keyboard and trackpad furiously. The screen flickers for a moment, and then the speakers suddenly explode with a painful volume of sound. Cameron flinches visibly at the aural onslaught. In his panicked key jabbing he apparently pushed the sound level up and he now he nervously fumbles with the laptop attempting to bring the sound back down to a normal level. We hear a voice with echo chamber effect yelling in the background, "What's the frequency Kenneth?" and then *Yakety Sax*, the music most commonly associated with *The Benny-Hill Show* pours out of the speakers while the images on the screen show a lampoon of news with re-cuts of 'actual' news: we see a presidential swearing-in ceremony spliced with all kinds of variations from an assassination during the event, like the president's head exploding into gore that splatters the camera lens and all the attendees on the stage with brain matter and blood. A title bar rolls out in the lower thirds that says, "The American Scream!" Several attendees dig their finger in the gore hanging from their faces and suits and taste it like they are wiping up some spilled food. They smile as they lick their lips. Cut to: the same swearing-in scene replayed but now with a grey alien being sworn in; then the same scene, but now the president-elect suddenly sprouts wings and bulging red eyes, and takes flight before a massive crowd on the lawn of the Washington Mall with the Washington Monument prominently visible in the background. The President-elect flies to the top of the monument and then takes a large bird-like dump on the crowds below who all hold up their hands, upturned faces smiling as they are covered in white and green bird-like shit.

Cameron finally manages to bring the sound levels back to humane decibels. He scrubs back through the video in search of the footage of the anchor he just watched, but all he can find is more of the same Presidential lunacy that we have been seeing on the screen. "No, this must be the wrong video," he stammers, "where is it?" he says in a panicky voice as he opens one video after another, only to discover that the video is no longer there. He finally plops down on the couch, and sits staring at a video of a football game, with the sound turned off, and just keeps staring blankly at the screen. Cameron turns off the laptop and then picks up a TV remote and clicks on the cable feed for the flat screen. He pulls a couch cushion over his head and with a normal cable TV news feed running as background noise.

He manages to shake off his distress enough to rise and walk slowly to the bathroom. He goes to the sink and vigorously washes and dries his face. Leaning on the sink, he leans toward the mirror, looking into his eyes with a searching expression. He flips a light switch, and the fluorescent lighting reluctantly buzzes and flickers on in a series of aborted strikes. In between flashes of light, his reflected image recedes into the silhouette of what looks like someone wearing a hoodie and aviator sunglasses. The two images alternate with increasing frequency as the overhead light cycles to equilibrium. We see the bulb finally turn on, emitting an audible "ding-" like sound. Instead of Cameron, the unidentified hooded person is the one left standing before the mirror. On the surface of the aviator lenses, two spinning hyperobjects of ungraspable geometry momentarily flash. They have edges and angles that one could only call "alien" as if they are pure thoughts brought to life in this time and space but still keeping one foot in another time and space. The geometry is non-Euclidian, with surfaces that can be focused on only momentarily, and then the perspectives shift as if they are purposefully sensing the viewer's focus and intention and then they retreat to a new configuration. In this aspect, they appear to be pure living forms, with surfaces that are not only alive in the usual sense of the concept but alive on levels and in a way that is ineffable. He picks up a stick of dark-red lipstick that is on the vanity counter and slowly presses it into the mirror to draw the Liminal symbol. Perspective shifts as we pull back to reveal that we were also seeing him through a mirror, inverting horizontal symmetry. Palming the lipstick, he walks through the apartment and turns left outside, all the while tracing the walls to his left with a red line, like a maze. Fade to black.

BLEED-OVER

We see Cameron, looking somewhat sloven, walking down the street, juggling his shoulder bag, cell phone and a cup of coffee. He is not doing this with much dexterity and eventually, he squeezes the paper coffee cup too hard, and the lid flies up, and coffee flies out and gets all over him and his devices. He flings the now mostly empty coffee cup in disgust. "Ah, shit," he says, shaking coffee off of the hand that formerly held the cup. He stands there, maybe a little too long and shakes his hand and keeps looking down at his now stained clothes when a man in a dark suit walks up behind him with his hand under his jacket as if he is reaching for a weapon. We pull back as we see what looks like a hit is about to happen to the hapless Cameron. The man pauses, then steps around Cameron, and moves rather impatiently past him on the sidewalk, breaking the tension of the moment. Cameron, who is engrossed in his coffee crisis, has been unaware of the menacing appearance of impending harm. The man is dressed in a 1950s style suit, with narrow lapels and narrow black tie, crisp white shirt and shiny black leather shoes. He has the look of a federal employee during the Kennedy era. He appears to have a shaved head, and his eyebrows are almost imperceptible. The suited man looks vaguely Eurasian in ethnic origin, although there is something off about him and one could not be specific if trying to identify him. As he walks past, we see something move under his jacket and around his torso. This catches Cameron's eye, and he does a double take. The man walks a few paces past Cameron and stops, adjusting something under his jacket, almost seeming to chase whatever it is around his torso like someone would chase a mouse or a bug that had crawled under their clothing. We see something appear for a second in the opening of the man's suit coat. It looks very similar to the hyperobjects we saw previously in the mirror episode that Cameron experienced earlier. Cameron sees this too. "Hey!" Cameron yells, suddenly. The man looks up with an eerily calm expression and looks at Cameron with dead eyes. He speaks, in a monotone voice.

"Yes? How can I be of assistance?" he intones, almost computer-like. Cameron grabs at the man's jacket, clumsily, while simultaneously trying to pocket his cell phone. The man deftly avoids Cameron's attempts to grab him.This results in a goofy circular dance with the man moving smoothly around like a cat and Cameron clumsily groping in the air for the lapel that keeps smoothly avoiding his grasp. Cameron catches a better glimpse the object now, revealing itself to be increasingly similar in look and qualities to the hyperobjects he saw reflected in the bathroom mirror. "Where did you get that?" Cameron says, somewhat hysterically, while still vainly grasping at the man's lapels. The man is still avoiding his attempts at restraint with the grace of a dancer. "That's proprietary IP!" Cameron yells, "did those fuckers in China sell that to you?" The man calmly and deftly grabs Cameron by the thumb of his right hand, which he made another vain and desperate grab with. The man bent Cameron's thumb back, with a swift and effortless motion. Cameron yelps with pain and drops to one knee. The man then slowly leads Cameron down to the sidewalk with his thumb, which is in some strange joint lock hold. He pulls Cameron all the way down until Cameron is laying on his side, whimpering on the sidewalk. Then, the man releases Cameron, points at him and in his monotone voice, says quietly, "Stay down." Cameron rolls his eyes up to look at the man but doesn't raise his head or move any other part of his body. He is whimpering, his nose has begun to run, and he sniffles to keep the snot from running out but is only partially successful. The man straightens up, adjusts his coat, and reaching under his jacket, makes a forceful movement as if he is locking something into place or holstering a weapon. He looks down at Cameron and says in his even tone, "I don't know what your problem is sir, but I suggest you get help. If I see you again and you approach me, I will restrain you more forcefully, and will be compelled to involve the authorities." The man brushes his jacket shoulders and sleeves, punctuating "That, will not, end well, for you," and then looks down at Cameron. "Do we understand each other?" "Yes-" Cameron sniffles, "I just thought I saw…" "You saw nothing," the man interrupts Cameron and then turns on his heel and walks away, stiffly. As he approaches a corner, he lifts a finger to his right ear and lifts his coat sleeve to his mouth before rounding the corner and disappearing from sight. Cameron is watching him depart and notices this movement. Slowly, Cameron sits up and with his arms tucked under his knees he gently rocks back and forth on the sidewalk, catching his breath. People walk around him, occasionally casting a furtive glance in his direction, before stepping around him. Occasionally we see a hyperobject darting just at the periphery of vision on various people's bodies as they walk by. Cameron notices this and sits and stares with an incredulous look on his face, staying in the same position. Eventually, a police cruiser does a slow roll-by, and Cameron sees them. He hastily stands up and dusts himself off before moving down the street casting glances over his shoulder at the two cops who are giving him a penetrating stare from inside the cruiser.

We are now at Cameron's house as he comes in the door, shaking the hand that was previously in a thumb lock as if trying to shake off the pain and numbness. The house is even more of a mess than the last time we saw it. He drops his bag heavily onto the couch and picks up his laptop from the coffee table. He wakes the computer up, and password unlocks it, then he brings up a GoMail page in his browser and begins typing an email to Gabe, which we can see on screen. The email is addressed to gabe@marketingwiz.com, and we see Cameron typing the following:

Gabe,

What the ever loving fuck? I see the 3D facsimiles all over this city. People are wearing them in public! They are animatronic (is that what they'd be called?). I mean they move. Or they are video projections or something because I saw several today and either you've lost track of your supply chain or your Chinese manufacturer has pirated my IP but either way, I NEED AN EXPLANATION NOW. This could ruin Liminal! Please email or call me ASAP.

He smacks the final keys with force and then hits send, and we hear a "whoosh" sound as the email is sent. He then opens a personal diary application called Diaryia, opens a new entry and begins typing.

"I saw something today, or I think I did, but to be sure and to be safe I am operating as if I did. I can't *be too cautious. If I did not see what I thought I saw and the hyperobject toys have not been pirated, what did I just see? Am I losing it? No! I won't think that way. Gabe isn't responding; maybe he thinks I'm overreacting, tool. I'll show him- I'll take some fucking pictures of what I'm seeing, let's see if he has anything to say about that. I have to be careful not to run into that finger-puppet ninja, can't be seen by him again, have to act covertly. And WTF was that about anyway? Maybe I should rent a little shitbox vehicle for recon. mission? If Maya ever found out I was going "Spenser'ish" I fear she would leave me. I can't say I would 100% blame her, but it would destroy me utterly. No, that's not what is going on. I must stop being stupid. I fucked up, and she is at her Mom's but she is coming back and what I saw was my IP that's been mishandled by motherfucking Gabe or pirated by motherfucking foreign interests. I saw things on the TV and in the mirror because I am stressed, lacking proper sleep and I miss Maya! Plus I've been drinking too much and smoking way too much of that boutique weed. I have to watch that stuff. It is strong. I will sort this out, and Maya will come home, and everything will go back to normal. Everything will work out. It will all*

work out."

INTENTIONAL GRAVITY

We are at Cameron's apartment now, and we see Cameron stepping outside. Only one solitary parked vehicle can be seen, and it's directly in front of his door. It's an old beat-up baby blue Honda Civic hatchback, low-slung and sporting tinted windows. With a puzzled look on his face, he walks up to the passenger-side door and stops. Confusion turns to curiosity. Furtively, he glances up and down the empty street. A narrow smile creeps across his face as he reaches for the chrome handle. Click, the door is unlocked. The car's interior is clean, not polished but also not displaying any sign of recent use. He pokes his head in and realizes that a screw-driver is jammed in the ignition, next to it a custom toggle-switch labeled "Relay." Cameron's smile widens to a demonic grin, and, without a second glance, he jumps into the car and over to the driver's seat. He flips the toggle, then grips the screwdriver underhanded and turns it. The car starts in first, leaping forward as the passenger door closes. Cameron, not missing a beat, shifts the car into second and peels-off down the street. He makes the first right turn and continues to drive in a quick serpentine pattern through various side-streets, driving evasively to cover his tracks.

Eventually, he checks and adjusts the rearview mirror, looking visibly relieved to find no one is following him. He passes a street sign indicating a 35Mph speed limit and winces when he sees the tachometer reading 65. Slowing down, he turns off the street and coasts onto a barely paved freeway underpass. We can hear his phone vibrating, "Yes Gabe?" Cameron says to himself as he pulls his phone out. The look of annoyance on his face turns to perplexity as we see his phone displays no recent calls or messages, "Huh?" Still looking at his phone, "Well, then, of..." A metallic thud interrupts him as he looks up to realize that he just nearly ran over a homeless-looking man, "Watch where you're going, fool!" the man says, shaking his fist at Cameron and punctuating his anger with another swing at the car. He bends down to pick up a brick as Cameron begins to say, "I'm so so–," remembering the tinted glass, he starts frantically turning the crank to roll down the driver-side window, just in time to say, "–so sorry!" Their eyes lock as we realize this is the same man we saw sitting next to Spencer at *The Heart of Darkness.* "Cameron?" he asks in amazement, beaming with a smile that makes the brick seem made of air when he lets it gently fall to the ground. Without saying another word, still smiling, he extends his arm to point-out a freeway support pillar, drawing a circle in the air with his finger to indicate what's behind it. Still silent, he makes a motion like depressing the shutter on a camera, then snaps an armed-forces salute. Cameron nods, returns the gesture and reaches for his phone on the passenger seat. He quickly pivots back to take a candid picture of the mysterious character, only to find him gone, "Of course!" Cameron exclaims like something is actually dawning on him, "to posterity then," he takes a picture of where the man used to be standing.

On the other side of the pillar, a large liminal sigil is painted between four smaller symbols at the corners of a centered-square configuration, with edge-length approximating the diameter of its subtended circle. Cameron lets the Civic slow to a stop. He tries to get out of the car, but the driver-side door won't budge, so he climbs out the window. Walking over to the pillar, he snaps a few photos of the whole configuration and then does close-ups of the four smaller symbols, which look like disguised AR codes or holographic binary interference patterns. A sound distracts Cameron, and he looks away as we see a faint red overlay on his phone's display scanning the images, without him noticing. As he pockets the phone, we see a flurry of small ethereal hyperobjects orbiting the device in a bloom of illuminated alien characters. The hyperobjects shootout in a tight finger-four formation, avoiding Cameron's line of sight as he walks toward the vehicle. They go to scan the same AR codes that Cameron just photographed, hovering in front of them. Bobbing in mid-air, they turn toward each other for a moment, each as though signaling approval to the other before shooting away in opposite directions faster than we can track them.

Back in the car, Cameron slowly drives along under the freeway taking a few more pictures of other liminal symbols found throughout before getting back on a side-street. An off-duty cop drives by in the opposite direction as Cameron turns onto the main artery where we can see *The Heart of Darkness* approaching from the distance. "Perfect!" he says out loud spotting a free parking space. He engages his signal and starts to turn when a white Range Rover pops out from a blind alley and snakes his spot. Visibly frustrated, Cameron sighs and guns it, accelerating rapidly to pass the vehicle and get back into the right lane. Again, after having signaled, just as he is turning left to zip back into traffic, a black Chevy Suburban from a car service also accelerates just enough not to let Cameron through. Cameron slams on the brakes as another errantly parking vehicle 50 yards ahead also chooses that exact instant to rapidly pull out and try again, turning the Chevy's possibly even unconscious micro-aggression into a potentially lethal situation. The Civic fishtails on the edge of losing control as time dilates, Cameron downshifts, steers hard and pumps the accelerator before releasing the clutch to shoot left, barely passing behind the Suburban and into an empty middle lane, "Way too close."

He drives up beside the Chevy for a few city blocks, unable to catch a glimpse of the driver through the car service's darkened windows. Cameron maintains an unnaturally constant distance from it in an attempt to disappear into its driver's blind-spot and mental periphery. He then alternates between slowly and imperceptibly drifting closer to it and performing overcorrected rapid turns towards the suburban, getting close enough to kiss the vehicle lightly. Each time, it's startled driver reacts in an increasingly panicked and erratic manner, showing a marked breakdown of confidence and decline of skill. "There we go, one less lesson, class over," Cameron concludes with a strange tinge of arrogance while pulling into the parking lot of the Cornucopia supermarket. As he turns into a free spot, the Civic suddenly dies, leaving him just enough momentum to perfectly roll into allotted space. "Weird," he says, repeatedly flipping the switch and turning the ignition to the now entirely unresponsive vehicle. He takes the opportunity to review the pictures he just took on his phone and shoot them over to Gabe as he smiles with satisfaction at the swoosh of delivery.

In the store, Cameron passes behind the checkout aisles as we hear *"Code two-hundred... Two-Oh-One"* crackle over the muzak before he goes up to a friendly-looking manager behind the register. "Psst," he asks in a strange sonorous cadence, "can I have the bathroom co-ode?" he says the word code, melodically, breaking into a smile. The manager complies, warmly adding, "For you? The world! It's a one and two together, three and four" They laugh, and Cameron smiles. On his way to opposite end of the store, he seemingly tries to rehearse some kind of retort as he mouths "It was always..." Passing the discount section, he presses the code on the bathroom's digital lock and opens the door to a clean and empty bathroom, "Ah, all mine!" he says with outstretched arms. Quasi-ceremoniously, like a disheveled king on his way to the coronation, he goes to wash his hands. Leaving the water on, he turns to the side suddenly, hands dripping like he was expecting someone to dry them, or, as though he were performing an interpretative dance move stuck between a very out-of-order impression of a robot and some dementedly inbred version of a zombie from *Thriller*. We see it appears that all three of the stalls, empty moments ago, have now been inexplicably occupied. "Fine," he says to himself, shaking the water off his hands, "Fuck-it..." Taking advantage of still running faucet, he gets up on his toes and pisses in the sink, "...Yes, I am king of the mainstream, assholes!" On his way out of the Cornucopia, he grabs a forty-ounce beer and slides it under his shirt while looking directly at the manager, who pretends not to notice.

Outside, before the sliding doors close behind him, a flicker of sadness passes across Cameron's face as we hear the intercom, "It's Kamron's last day today..." sounding much less rehearsed than the previous broadcast. Cameron says, trying to reassure himself, "you always see them again... that last check." From above, we spot the previous four hyperobjects tracking Cameron in a slow-moving spinning circle formation, with him at its center. This mirrors a prank someone played in the parking lot while Cameron was inside, connecting all the shopping carts together end-to-end to make an ouroboros of empty consumption. Smiling, he jumps back into the Civic and tries to start it again. It compiles, and Cameron laughs, "Of course!" As before, the hyperobjects scatter into the LA skyline.

CONFRONTATION CALLS

We see Cameron sitting in front of his computer, reading a forum called ReadIt, scrolling through the threaded conversation and staring at the screen with a look of serious intensity. We see a sampling of the posts scrolling next to the figure of Cameron scrolling.

DonnieDongle: "...and then after I started playing Liminal, people who I didn't even know started calling me Cameron. I mean, I understand we gave our intimate details to the game curators so that our experience would be intimate and personalized, but honestly, it boggles my mind to think that hired actors follow me around in public.

FoxyFaust: "@DongleDangle, do u leave the location feature turned on on your phone?"

DonnieDongle: "Yes, and now that you mention it, I guess that could explain it. Still, they must have a lot of people in the field to be able to intercept me like that."

Cameron scrolls some more.

Oscar_Mayer_Winner: "Has anyone else been seeing the Liminal logo stenciled on the sidewalks and walls? How do they not get fined for graffiti? Do you think they have permission or do they just go total Banksy?"

He continues to scroll.

Sidewaze: "This reminds me of that Jejune game in SF. There were people on conspiracy boards screaming about their posters and flyers, thinking it was some sort of cult actually out to get them. You have to hand it to the Liminal people; they really have come up with the perfect immersive game environment. The entire world is the gameboard. It's sheer genius!"

He stops scrolling and looks out the window thoughtfully. Suddenly his cell phone rings, and he starts, jolted from his reverie. He looks at the screen and sees, "Maya" displayed along with a picture of Maya smiling into the camera, cuddling a Hello Kitty doll next to her cheek. "Hello?" he answers the phone, his voice noticeably excited. We hear Maya on the other end of the call. "Hi, Cameron." She says, her tone is cautious but not hostile or cold. "How are you?" she asks after a beat or silence. "I'm good," Cameron says, while absentmindedly continuing to scroll through the ReadIt forum. "I'm looking forward to you coming home in a few days." "Yeah," she replies. After a slight pause, she adds, "Me too. Me too, really. I'm sorry we fought. I know you've been under a lot of pressure with your investors to perform and I overreacted..." "I was an idiot," he interrupts. "I should not have said the stupid things I said, and I should not have let work wind me up so much, I let it cause me to react in anger. I swear, I will time-out myself in the future instead of lashing out." You can hear Maya audibly sigh on the other end of the phone. "That goes for both of us," she replies. "Although..." she begins then stops. "Yes?" Cameron says after she pauses. "I have to ask," she begins again, "am I walking into a bachelor's disaster when I come home?" she queries, and then quickly adds, "I just want to know what to expect," Cameron looks around at the house which is clearly a housekeeping nightmare. He slowly pushes some ashes and takeout detritus into a waste can that is next to his desk. "Oh, no," he says, in an almost unbelievable exaggerated voice, trying to sound innocent and thereby sounding guilty. "Ok," Maya says "I'm sorry, I just had to ask." Cameron looks around with a very guilty and somewhat panicked look on his face. "Uh, yeah," he says, "I get it." after a second he goes back to scrolling through the forum. "So, I'm picking you up at the airport day after tomorrow?" he asks "Yes," Maya answers. "and don't worry, I didn't tell my parents anything. No need dragging them into this. Besides, we're fine now, right?" She accentuates the word, "right" as if to confirm that they are both on the same page on this issue. "Yes, yes. 100%" Cameron says, still looking at the forum. His scrolling has slowed now, and he is clearly reading something on the forums. "Ok hon, I have to run some numbers before I make my investor call-in today, so I should go. I'm looking forward to seeing you. Love you" he says. His physical posture indicates that he is distracted, but his voice is deceptively not giving this fact away. "Ok, babe. Me too. Love you. Bye." "Bye," Cameron says while leaning in closer to the screen. He flicks his finger across the screen to flip off the call and slowly lays the phone down on the desk. He has an intense look on his face. We see the forum text on screen now.

TheRealCameron: "Liminal has always been here will always be here. The door was opened as was always planned and as it will always be planned. i am legion because i am many. i am many because i am one. Marduk is the one. one is the arousal of the monad from the void which is zero and zero is Tiamat. The great dragon goddess who precedes creation and creation is a lie because it is really only the reordering of the void after she had been slain into numbers, parts, because the void, the useful part of a vessel which is its emptiness, which was a whole as emptiness, has been rendered asunder, taking the purity of the void, the great pre-Kabbalistic zero and made the vessel into the broken pottery shards we now call reality. There are many Cameron's and one Cameron. Liminal the game has infected you through interaction with its creepypasta and memes, Liminal the game is the game that is not a game. It plays you by making you think it plays you. Have you met the men in suits? They are not from here.

They are from the void and only have one foot in this reality."

Cameron now has a look on his face like that of a cornered animal. A line of sweat has formed above his upper lip, and he wipes it off with his forefinger. He continues to read,

"They are the physical manifestations of the artifacts, talked about in the game documents. As much as you may think these are facsimiles that have been created for this game, you are wrong. They are manifestations of hyperobjects, coaxed into this reality from another, with human form outgrowths to aid in their camouflage, until the time of their maturation. How do I know all of this?"

The text is now at the bottom of the screen. Cameron holds his breath as he scrolls down to reveal more text. After some blank space looking as if someone hit enter a few times after the last entry, there is a small block of text that reads,

"Because i created this game. Because i coaxed the objects over. Because i am Cameron, the real creator of this game and if you are playing this game i am slowly becoming you becoming me now too. Because i am the irreducible element, the essence of something beyond the parts that can be quantified and reduced and categorized. I am that which precedes all that. Because i know you are reading this right now, Cameron."

Cameron is now wild-eyed and breathing somewhat heavily. He stands and yells at the monitor, "No, no, no, no! Fuck you!" and he grabs the laptop and flings it against the wall. He then kicks it across the room, all the while still screaming, "Fuck you, fuck you, fuck you, you gaslighting..." he pauses, as if to ponder exactly who he wants to blame and then failing to come up with anything, finishes by yelling, "...gaslighters!" He then sits down in the office chair heavily, covers his face and begins to sob. The sobbing slowly morphs into maniacal laughter, and as he uncovers his face, we see that his expression has become a mask of pure madness. His face shifts and becomes a mask of sadness again and he sobs, he shifts and laughs, and this shifting continues until we fade out on him sobbing.

LIMINAL ANSWERS

Cameron is wearing his messenger bag which is overflowing with papers and random wires such as USB cables and charger cords. He seems to be juggling, with a herculean effort, the simple tasks of extracting his keys from his pocket, pulling his phone from the overflowing messenger bag, and opening the storm door that opens onto the front door of his apartment, all at the same time. He somehow manages to make this all look complicated and difficult beyond measure. He seems flustered, and his face is red, and a few veins bulge from the effort of this seemingly simple set of tasks. He is yelling into his phone's headset, "Spencer, I'll call you back, I really need to clean this house before Maya gets home or I-am- a- dead- man!" he pauses after each one of those last five words. He drags his thumb across the screen to hang up the call, all the while he is dropping the phone into his pocket, juggling the jingling key ring in search of the proper key and opening the storm door with his left foot. As he pushes the key into the front door lock, the door unexpectedly swings inward, indicating that it is not locked. Cameron stands for a second, taking this in, and then he pushes the door the rest of the way open with his foot. We see inside the house now and inside is a figure, their back turned to Cameron, apparently oblivious to his presence. The person is wearing a green hoodie, and they turn for a sec, and we catch a glimpse of a profile, enough to deduce that it is a bearded man, wearing aviator glasses. He has his hood drawn so we can't see much more of his head. He is flipping through a stack of papers, flipping them and letting them fall one by one to the floor as he scans them as if he is in search of something. The rest of the apartment looks as if it has been rifled noticeable even through Cameron's slovenly methods of housekeeping. The man stops and then spins around to face Cameron. We see a smile slowly creep across his face. Cameron drops his keys and shrugs off his messenger bag. "Oh, boy. Did you pick the wrong day and wrong person to pull this shit on!" He growls, as a slightly unhinged look comes across his face, he leers with a lewd-looking grin that more resembles a grimace, and he suddenly charges the man. Surprisingly, the man does not flee, but almost in a mirror image of Cameron's charge, he too has charged at Cameron. The two men meet in the middle of the living room and with a meaty "whomp!" they collide chest first and bounce off each other. Both regain composure, and they charge each other again, each one moving in almost a mirror image of the other. The two men warily circle each other, each trying to be agile and cat-like but instead coming off as two not very agile people trying to appear agile. It's almost comical if not for the seriousness of the situation. Suddenly, Cameron quickly drops and swiftly snatches up a TV remote that was laying on the floor. He throws it in a manner that shows a form of a non-athlete. However, the throw is sufficiently hard enough and on target and hits the hooded man square on the bridge of his nose. Blood begins to gush from the man's wound, and he puts his hand to his wound and then withdraws it to see blood. A shocked look comes across what we can see of his face. Cameron screams in a hysterical voice. "Got you fucker! This is my house, mother fucker! My- mother- fucking- house!" He begins to move forward towards the man but slips on a paper plate that has a half-eaten slice of pizza stuck to it. The plate and its contents look several days old. Cameron stumbles but doesn't go down. While he struggles to regain his balance, the hooded man, still holding his hand over his bleeding wound, sees his opening and darts out the open front door. Cameron, slipping and dodging his way through the cluttered living room takes off in pursuit.

The man has a lead of 10-15 feet. They run, cutting across streets and through traffic, knocking over garbage cans, running into and around pedestrians, causing dogs to bark in yards they pass, and even setting off a parked car's alarm as they both scramble over the hood. The chase goes on for several blocks, and Cameron is never able to catch the man. Cameron comes close a few times, but the hooded man always seems to stay just out of reach. As the chase progresses, we see that they are moving into an area that is devoid of people and the buildings all seem to be under construction or in various states of demolition. The hooded man gains a longer lead, and then he turns a corner, and as Cameron rounds the corner in pursuit, he sees that the man has disappeared. He stops running and, gasping for breath, leans over and places his hands on his knees, while warily scanning the surrounding area in search of the man. He is nowhere in sight. The surrounding area is empty, no people or activity of any kind can be detected. The air is silent. Cameron pulls the cellphone out of his pocket and dials 911. He is met with the three tones that you receive when you dial a number that has been disconnected. We hear a recorded voice that says all circuits are busy. He sighs and pushes the phone back in his pocket. He stands, still catching his breath and leans over with his hands back on his knees. Suddenly, Cameron is startled by the ringing of the cellphone in his pocket. He stands upright quickly and in a sort of frantic series of motions digs the cellphone out of his pocket and answers the call, holding the phone up to his head. "Hello," he says into the phone, his voice wavering, his mouth still open with silent gasps. We hear a voice on the other end of the call. It is a man's voice, kind of snarky in tone, but somehow familiar. "Did you call 911?" the voice says, "Yes," Cameron replies, taking a big gulp and controlling his breathing. "But how did you know?" he asks, "We receive a callback signal when a 911 call does not go through, or there's a hang-up. Just one more service of your wonderful telecommunications industry and the ever watchful eye of law enforcement!" the man's voice projects facetiousness. "By the way, who do you think you are anyway? Captain America" he adds, with an audible snort at the end. "Wait, what?" Cameron says, confused. "Chasing that guy like that. How did you know he didn't have a gun or a knife or maybe he was leading you back to his friends, the way a coyote will lure a town dog back to the pack?" "The wha- how the hell do you know, wait- who the fuck is this?" Cameron babbled out, his face turning red. He turned around in all directions, looking in vain for someone or something that would explain this situation. "Even Mark Twain knew about the coyotes, you rube." the man laughed. "Never, ever, ever leave the boat. Tigers! Never follow a coyote out of the SUV, town dog! Trickster food!" the voice on the other end was now laughing in a way that made Cameron's eyes bulge out and his face to go red. "Stay down." the voice suddenly said, going monotone. "Wait, you! You're that guy!

How did you intercept my call? What the..." but the phone call has gone dead. "Hello! Hello?" Cameron shouts. He starts to throw his phone but then stops himself. He stands looking dazed and he continues to peer around as if looking for someone who was observing him in secret. Finally, he stops looking and then he stands still for a few more seconds, looking very confused. He lifts the phone, dials a number and waits. "Hello? Spencer? I need to talk to you about something. In private. No, now. Ok, I'm on my way."

SPENCER'S WAY

Cameron turns onto an empty street and walks up to an intercom to press the last and only unlit button, faintly reflecting the glow of an ancient sodium lamp. We pull back to see Spencer's apartment building is a repurposed multi-story factory. It has a loading-level freight elevator with the word 'FABRIC' printed across it in what looks like very old, sunbaked and peeling paint, followed by '(-)Height' in fresh graffiti. Above the building's second floor cornice, the word 'TEXTILE' is written to span most of the street-facing facade. The signage is made out of what look like ceramic tiles, adorned by flourishes of street-art borrowing heavily from M.C. Escher's *Reptile* tessellations. Cameron is already trying to fish a nylon strap from between the freight elevators parting doors in order to pull them open when the door-buzzer sounds to let him into the stairwell. He is about to get in the elevator when he says out loud, "Eh, no!" With a look of relief, he turns to hastily make his way down the stairwell to Spencer's apartment. We see Cameron through the spyglass before Spencer lets him in.

Inside, Spencer's apartment is surprisingly well appointed with artifacts and matching decor from around the world; all very well put together. "I'm always very pleasantly surprised by how much more neat and well-traveled you are–" Cameron says, trying to minimize and shift focus from his own current state of disarray. Spencer interjects, "–and we'll leave it at that to keep it as a compliment, thank you. Now, what's up man, I'm a little worried about you." Cameron sits down and continues, "Yeah, you and me both, but what's this again with your getting all uptight about your gift for interior, 'design,' let's call it?" "Look," Spencer says becoming suddenly quite still, "I understand that you're having a hard time," his demeanor changing into a more uncharacteristically commanding tone, "but there's really no reason for us to go there right now." Cameron, apparently genuinely confused, issues a reluctant, "W-T-F, mate?" He seems disoriented like he finally realizes how lost he must be. Spencer gives him a look of mixed surprise and disbelief, "Wait, wait, wait," he asks, lighting a cigarette, "bro., how long have you known me?" Somewhat nonplussed, Cameron returns, "c'mon Spence, I don't know, more than a few years now must be, what's–."

Spencer interrupts him again, distractedly thumbing his temple as though just now remembering something he always forgetting, "–ah, see, somehow it appears you are not registering that one time, not too long ago, someone took it upon themselves to get way too concerned about me, one might say more than was entirely necessary or even proper. That brave soul then went above and beyond the call of duty with a campaign to raise awareness of how I may have been, allegedly, a danger to myself and others." Waving his free hand demonstratively with a presentational flourish, he continues, "Ergo, the focus on at least *appearing* sane." He takes a long drag off the cigarette, which he holds awkwardly. Calming down, he drops the facade, with a tempered welcoming of vulnerability, "By then, practically everyone I knew suddenly acted like my being bat-shit crazy had always been some foregone conclusion, just like that. I had become the local cautionary tale that parents warn their children of in hushed tones when you pass them on the street. That'll make you feel like acting-out, big time.

Double down, I always say. Things got out of control. So, I was held for observation, courtesy of L.A. County." Cameron seems at a loss for words, so Spencer continues. "Yeah, so first they thought I was their everyday fifty-one-fifty, standard fare, seventy-two-hour weekend trip kind of thing. Then they upped me to a fifty-two-seventy, the works, more than a month paid vacation. Lots of time to think." Cameron betrays the shadow of a smile as he finally gets his words back, "And there I was, thinking that thinking was what first got me into this mess." They laugh, then Spencer

qualifies "maybe, hold on a second..."

He extinguishes his cigarette and walks over to a poster on the opposite

wall, "See this, *recognize* it?" Squinting, Cameron answers, "Eh, yes, I

think... That's that illustration thingie of Hobbes' *Leviathan.* The body

politic, absolute leader, controls his subjects as articulations of himself.

Like the Yakuza, you cut off your finger when you mess-up, to *remember*

your place in the order of things–" "–Sure," Spencer reels him back in,

"now, look closer." We see that the multitude of individuals making up the

whole are actually monstrous composites of other various animals, turning

the body politic into a horrifying bestiary with only the most distant

resemblance to anything human. In a tone of mixed condescension and

resignation, Spencer slaps the poster as though to try and concretize or

reify his point. "This," slapping the poster even harder, "this particular

process right here is based on visual perception. It uses an algorithm

trained to recognize and identify images and runs it backward. Instead of

moving toward a unity of different identifying features, it takes various

disparate elements and overdetermines them in isolation." He cocks his

head at Cameron who silently nods to indicate that he is at least partially

following. Spencer continues, "Without taking into account surrounding

features in order to synthesize a coherent, inherently unified whole, it

creates monsters by drilling down into different parts and reinforcing elements that are at odds with each other. Ringing any bells?" A pained grimace stretches across Spencer's face as he pauses before saying, "Now, imagine this being run not against visual perception, instead, it's based on identifying the core values and belief systems that inform human behavior.

Targeting indeterminate areas of our concerns and beliefs, it turns them into something else by modifying the spin on the information it provides us surrounding those issues. It finds ambiguities, inconsistencies or biases in our thinking to predict our susceptibility to particular programming– 'semiotic driving'. Then, it divides us against ourselves and others, altering our thoughts and behavior without allowing us to recognize what is happening. Divide and conquer. Because it is modeled on and outclasses our recognition system, it knows how to manipulate us so that we never even realize how it's happening!" Cameron, somewhat at a loss though genuinely trying to connect responds, "From what I gathered, and what you're saying this *thing,* it's messing with our expectations, steering us off-course. The whole driving thing, like in a car, by moving us, it's learning how to drive itself. Or at least drive us insane? I mean, I think that I actually do get what you're saying. Do I?"

Spencer takes a breath from his long-winded and rambling discourse and Cameron seizes that opportunity to take the floor. "Look, Spence, I get that you've been dipping into the edibles and want to engage me in some perverse intellectual conversation, as usual, but I have some real-world problems here, and I need your unique set of life experiences and outlooks to bounce off of for some perspective." He waits to see how Spencer will receive this, and not seeing any pushback, he continues. "I have been experiencing some very weird shit lately. I mean weird with a capital W. So weird in fact that it has me questioning my sanity. I thought since you have some experience with that kind of thing, you might be able to provide some perspective." he pauses and then adds, "No offense, of course." Spencer looks at him quizzically and then says, in a regular tone, his professorial voice now gone, "None taken. How can I help?" Cameron sighs with relief and then begins, "It all started, I think, when I released Liminal. I started- people started calling me- I saw, I see- things. I don't even know where to start." Cameron hangs his head and looks dejected. "At the beginning," Spencer says, "Start at the beginning." Cameron stands up and walks around, pacing and then sitting down and then swiftly standing up and pacing again as he relates the events of the last several days. We see this as a time lapse, with Cameron gesticulating wildly at times and Spencer appearing to ask questions, while the sound we hear in the foreground is a scratchy radio transmission, of what sounds like a numbers station. The music in the background is Mahler's Symphony Number 1 in D Major. Over the Mahler is a woman's voice, very even and slow, very melodic. She is speaking English, but she has a French accent. She is saying, "Twelve thirty-six, Subject, Cameron.

Forty-two sixteen, Iteration, two point three. Five eleven, bug reported. Sixteen fourteen nine, exploit incubation two-thirds compiled. Eleven eleven, handshake imminent." A radio conversation between two men overtakes the woman's speech. One of the men sounds like the MIB/911 operator, and the other man has a Russian accent. They are both speaking English. "Do you think he knows?" 911 guy asks. "Na," the Russian accented man says, "Not about the Liminal group, nyet." "Then how did he write about us? Is that part of the bleed he precipitated when he used the code we left on the honeypot site?" Mister 911 replied, "Da" Russian man replies, "The synchronicity factor is very much higher, even more, higher than the metamachine experiments of the 90s. Is to be expected, the unexpected when we open these doors. We only wish to open doors. Expectations of controlling what comes out? This is sure to lead to disappointment." "If we can't control it, why do it?" 911 asks, rather sharply, "Because we are the Liminal Group and we facilitate the unexpected. No more, No less." the squelch lowers, and static interspersed with various other competing broadcasts drown out the conversation. We come back to Cameron and Spencer sitting and facing each other.

Spencer looks long and hard at Cameron, before saying, "First off, I think someone hijacked your 911 call using a Stingray. The FBI has had this tech for a while but so have a lot of other non-state actors. Why they did it to you is another question." he pauses, "Where exactly- no, wait, let me rephrase that-" he stops and rubs the bridge of his nose for a second while closing his eyes, "what, exactly did you embed into the text of this game?" Cameron pauses and looks at Spencer for a few seconds without saying anything. The ticking of a computer drive being accessed can be heard in the background, while Spencer waits for his answer. "I found some documents on a Tor exit node that talked about semantic or semiotic driving," Cameron replied, rather slowly and deliberately. Spencer's eyebrows shot up. "That's kinda advanced for you isn't it?" he asked incredulously. "I had help," Cameron answered, energetically. "Plus, I heard a podcast about it." he finished. "So, basically, you were pawing through the document transfers of people who thought they were sending stuff safely," Spencer said, without hiding the disapproval in his voice. "Look," Cameron shot back, "I was looking for some of the same information you have heard about, but rather than just trading copypasta and speculation, I went looking for the real deal or at least to find out if it was real. It's a method that makes text and the concepts in the text highly memetic, kind of addicting. I thought it would enhance the playability of the game." "Oh, it's more than that!" Spencer shot back. "A lot more!" "What do you mean?" Cameron asked "Have you not heard of the Orange Soda experiment? A code name of course, but it was a language virus that's embeddable into regular text, a meta-algorithm of sorts, but it got out of the control of the Soviet team that developed it. Some say the virus actually developed some kind of meta-intelligence. It's all beyond me really, but basically, it became embedded in their minds, informed their internal narrative and drove them all insane. The government ended up sealing them all up in the facility until they had killed each other off in the throes of their madness. They had to cut all telecom in and out of the facility, and the soldiers they sent to keep the people inside wore ear coverings. They were instructed not to read anything like signs or notes that the people inside may hold up to the windows. There are people out there, former Soviet scientists familiar enough with that story and the method used, who have reported signs of the virus showing up in creepypasta and memes." he took a long breath and then continued. "They call it the Burroughsian Variant of Benway 2332." "Wait, what is this thing?" Cameron interrupted Spencer. "Spencer took a long audible breath, "Ok, crash course version," he said, opening a browser on his laptop and navigating to Wikipedia, "Ewan Cameron" Spencer says as the Wikipedia page loads on the large monitor in front of them, "Head of more professional psychiatric organizations than you can shake a stick at and also the verified, documented head of MKUltra." "Cameron?" Cameron mumbles, "Wait, MKUltra, you're saying that is real? I thought that was something the conspiracy crowd made up-" "Wrong" Spencer cuts him off. "While it is true that the information has been sensationalized and conflated with paranoid fantasies, I assure you, there was an actual MKUltra project, and it was pretty gruesome. The short story here is Cameron used drugs and tape loops in an effort to control behavior. He called his method, psychic driving." Spencer flips the browser to a Wikipedia entry for William S. Burroughs. "William Burroughs, experimental author, and all-around bright guy, who through his writings tried to warn us all of the existence or at least at the time he was writing the possibility of language viruses. Consequently, the usual suspects of lettered agencies were very interested in Burroughs' work." Now to Alfred Korzybski, himself a big influence on Burroughs and the father of General Semantics." The screen now showed the Wikipedia page for Korzybski. "Short story again, is among his theories was the idea that changes in language patterns can influence or even affect changes in human behavior. Of course, the Soviets and a few American-companies are currently using an amalgam of these ideas stirred in with some of the modern semiotic thinkers and the ideas of people like Clotaire Rapaille, who perfected methods that allows advertising to access the reptilian brain, and brother that's deep access. Tests like MyFace's humiliating 'mood experiments' are only a smokescreen." The browser flipped again now to Clotaire Rapaille's Wikipedia page. Spencer pauses and looks at Cameron to see if he's following, and sees a look of disbelief on Cameron's face. "When you're that deep, you're playing with forces usually only accessible through the collective unconscious, and now we're talking some heavy Jungian shit. What comes walking out of that doorway when you open it is anyone's guess, but now we're talking about opening doors to Lovecraftian realms, and all bets are off." The browser was now displaying a Wikipedia page for the concept of "emergence" Cameron was looking at Spencer now like he was insane. "So, you're saying that I used some infected text methodology that has allowed Liminal to become..." he paused as he considered what he was about to say. "...self-aware? Do you have any idea how batshit crazy that sounds?" Spencer snorts. "Yeah, laugh if you want, but you're the one here, now, telling me your life has turned into a Cronenberg film. Ever heard of The King in Yellow?" "The what?" Cameron asks, "Never mind. Anyway, I didn't say self-aware. This thing is probably primal or instinctual in nature, truly like a virus with a very rudimentary set of commands, survive, replicate, etc. I'm guessing it functions above the actual data, more like meta-data, drawing from and controlling data sets without actually being a part of them. This of course on some very meta-Hegelian level allows it to control perception. It is in hacker terms, an exploit of the Habitus Rex. The spell of the mind that tells you how to feel and what's real." he pauses. "And what's not. Not to go all Jim Carrey on you, but-" he continues after a pregnant pause. "I know you read Levenda's *Sinister Forces* when you were going through your conspiracy research phase for Liminal, and I'm not dismissing his unreliability due to the Simonomicon stuff, but he did hit on something when he made a case for a very ancient and very embedded evil force that can be coaxed out of hiding with the right- or wrong set of circumstances." "You know, Spence, sometimes even I don't know what the fuck you're talking about." Spencer looks straight at Cameron, "That's ok, you can always use Google, right?" they both stay silent for a few seconds, pondering the implications of Spencer's propositions. "Ok," Cameron finally says, after the pause, apparently ignoring the Google jab, "let's say, let's just say for the sake of argument that something— that what's happening— has *something* to do with my poor choices in using questionable sourced memetic hooks," he emphasizes the word something when he says it, to highlight that he isn't completely buying Spencer's proposition. "Maybe, just maybe, everything I am experiencing is some kind of gaslighting by some sort of— I dunno, agency that has recognized what I borrowed..." "Stole," Spencer interrupts "stole, just call a spade a spade." "Ok, took without permission," Cameron continues "Same as stole. Same thing." Spencer interjects again. "WHATEVER!" Cameron continues emphatically, "Can you at least concede that it's more of a probability that my scenario of a three-letter agency of some sort is behind this rather than leaping to the conclusion that this is all due to some sort of uber-consciousness arising from the text of a goddamn story?" Cameron was clearly agitated by Spencer's proposition. Clearly, this idea has provoked him somehow. "Look," Spencer says, "we can work with that model if that makes you more comfortable." he smiles at Cameron in a mildly condescending way, "Let's say for the sake of argument that your appropriation" he accents the word appropriation and makes air quotes as he does, still smirking. Cameron looks at him with a sour expression on his face. Spencer continues, "that your appropriation has been noticed. It's possible. It could be one of ours, one of theirs or one of someone else's."

"You mean, agencies? Yeah, now that makes more sense. I assume this Orange Soda experiment did not go unnoticed by various intelligence agencies around the world," he makes air quotes when he says Orange Soda, and he and Spencer both smile, the tension in the room breaking now. "Yeah," Spencer replies, "my sources say that the Americans and the Chinese were squirming like a geek boy at E3 when they heard about the alleged method to weaponize words. I'm sure the Langley boys sprayed their shorts when they verified that something or other had actually gone down at the institute. Just like the remote viewing race we got into with the Soviets, I doubt that the veracity of the program's results was the primary concern. SOMETHING went down, something went very, very wrong and much like the remote viewing programs, how much was real and how much was propaganda is debatable. There? Do I sound sane enough for you now?" Spencer smirks. "Yeah," Cameron replies, a tinge of relief in his voice "You do sometimes lead with the most improbable of the possibilities, Spence." "Oh, well, Occam's Razor aside my friend, you do understand that this still leaves you in the unenviable position of having one or several international intelligence agencies seeking your hide." Cameron is silent; an ashen look comes over his face. "Lucky me." he says glumly. "Spencer," he asks, "what got you through your hard times? I mean when your friends and family had you committed-" Spencer visibly winces when Cameron says "committed." "Honestly," Spencer says, with a very serious tone, "The only way out is through." "What?" Cameron asks, "The only way out is through. I had to resign myself to the journey. Like Joe Campbell's intrepid hero of a thousand faces, you have to own it. Realize you cannot turn back. You've crossed the Rubicon. No do-overs. Just ride the ride, as Hunter said, you buy the ticket; you ride the ride. While I could have argued that I didn't buy that ticket, as you might argue and deceive yourself into thinking, that gets you nowhere. You bought it- I bought it- somehow on some level, so buckle in and take it to the end. It's only struggling against it and grasping on to the notion that IF ONLY, you can somehow turn back and arrive somehow back where you started, that's what causes the discomfort. Ever notice how there's happy crazy people and unhappy crazy people? The unhappy ones are the ones who are uncomfortable with the notion that they're crazy. The happy ones are the ones who do not have any fucks left to give and therefore, they have accepted their fate." "Jesus fucking Christ, mister Buddha!" Cameron blurts out. "Yeah, but you know I'm right." Spencer says. Cameron looks at him sideways for a minute. Then his eyes grow wide, and then he pulls out his phone. "Fuck me, oh fuck me." he wails. "I was supposed to pick up Maya from the airport! Oh, fuck me-" he stands up and says hastily, "Thanks for everything Spence but oh my god, I have six messages from Maya, and she arrived at the airport over 2 hours ago. How the fuck could i have forgotten?" "Go," Spencer says, motioning at the door. "Go" Cameron rushes out the door, whispering "Oh fuck, oh fuck-" When he is gone,

Spencer stares at the door for a few seconds and then says out loud, "You poor, clueless bastard."

LOSING MAYA

Cameron rushes up the steps of his apartment, tripping on a few stairs as he ascends. He's fishing in his pockets for something, and very out of breath. As he approaches the front door, he notices it is still open from when he chased the burglar. The look on his face becomes one of concern, and he barges into the foyer of the apartment, calling out Maya's name in a panicked tone. "Maya! Maya! May-" he immediately falls over two suitcases that are sitting in the doorway that leads from the foyer into the interior of the apartment. He lands on the hardwood floor with a resounding thud and rolls into a sitting position. Maya is standing in the middle of the living room, looking around, taking in the wreckage of the apartment. We see the lipstick scrawls on the walls, marker scribbles on mirrors, papers and half-eaten takeout food scattered everywhere. There are a few holes in a few walls at the mid-shin level, as if they had been kicked. Several couch cushions have been pulled off the couch and along with a dirty sheet, form what looks like a makeshift bed next to the wall. Maya has a look of horror on her face. She turns to Cameron with her arms held slightly away from her body, hands pointed down, palms facing him as if to ask, "Why?" She now has a pleading look on her face. "I meant to pick you up!" Cameron stammers. "I really-" Maya makes a slicing motion in the air with her hand as if to say, "Stop!" she still has not spoken, and from the look on her face it appears she has been rendered speechless. Cameron begins again, "we had a break-in-" he says, standing up slowly. Maya levels her gaze at him as if to encourage him to go on and explain the surrounding disaster. "It's been insane," Cameron continues, "people have been following me, and the facsimiles were pirated and I think I accidentally used some secret Soviet project code in the game and then..." he pauses for breath and looks at her with an expression that implies that he is searching for her reception of this information, "No, let me start again-" he says, after pausing and not receiving any feedback from Maya other than a steely gaze that has not wavered. "I jumped a guy who was tossing our house in search of- well, I'm not sure of what-" he stopped and seemed to be thinking hard about what to say next. Maya still stood in the center of the room, arms now folded across her chest, expression unchanged. She cocked her head slightly to the right, as if to say, "and?" "People have been calling me Cameron, and I've been assaulted by men in suits that are either working for some government or came through a portal from the liminal realm or is it the imaginal realm?" He sits back down on the floor after blurting this out as if saying all of this out loud has sapped him of his energy. When he says all of this her expression finally changes. She raises one eyebrow, and a look of sadness comes across her face. She looks at him as if she pities him. "So, people have been calling you, Cameron?" she asks, in a somewhat delicate tone. "Yes!" he says, his face lighting up. happy that he has finally received some response from her. She looks at him a long time and then says, slowly, "I am going to leave now." she points to her bags still on the floor. "I called a Youber before you walked in. When I saw this-", she motions around the room with a look of disbelief on her face. "I knew that we have bigger problems than your occasional lapses of respect for me-" her face sags with sadness as she anticipates what is about to happen, "and now you tell me all of this-" she sighs, "I think you need to get help. Serious help. I can't be here to watch you destroy yourself like this. I will support you, but I can't be here and watch this go on. This has been going on too long." "Wait. What?" Cameron says, standing up again. "Going on too long? This all just started happening when I launched the game, wha-" "Cameron!" Maya screams, startling Cameron, causing him to jolt visibly. "This has been going on for almost a year! You lost the game to the investors when you couldn't stay focused, and when you started all of this aberrant behavior!" Cameron didn't seem to be listening closely anymore. "What did you call me?" was all he could ask "Your goddamned fucking name!" she suddenly stopped and stood erect. "Cameron, I love you, loved you, I don't know, I loved who you were, but I can't-do this anymore, I can't, we can't-" Cameron is standing with his arms hanging limply by his sides, with a wounded and confused look on his face. Outside a car, horn can be heard honking, and the sound of a phone vibrating in Maya's pocket can be heard at the same time. Maya whisks by Cameron, quickly pecking him on the cheek, scoops up her two bags and walks out the door. As she exits, she stops for a second and says, "I hope you seek the help you need." Cameron momentarily recovers from his shock and yells back, "How cliché!" We hear Maya walk down the stairs and then we hear a car door open and close and the sound of a car driving away. Cameron stands stock-still this entire time. He finally sits down on the floor again and begins to sob, uncontrollably while hugging his knees and burying his face in the crook of his arms.

THE HEART OF DARKNESS REDUX

We see a very disheveled Cameron walking across a busy city street. He is red-eyed as if he has been crying. He is dodging traffic rather unsuccessfully, narrowly missing being run over by several cars. A few of the cars honk their horns. One driver yells out of his passenger window, "Get out of the road, asshole!" Cameron seems oblivious to the danger of the situation. He absentmindedly drags his hand across the hood of the last car to screech to a halt in the path of his zig-zag route. The driver honks and throws his hands up in a WTF salute. As Cameron drifts out from in front of the car, the driver peels off in frustration. We now see Cameron is in front of the Heart of Darkness, but it looks very different. The sign is still above the storefront, and still, reads "The Heart of Darkness," but the front of the building has drastically changed. The large front windows are now covered over with some kind of tinted film, obscuring the view into the interior. Outside the building, various people lounge against the wall, to the left of the main entrance. The entrance now has a turnstile in front of it guarded by a large man with long hair and a t-shirt advertising a death metal band. Groups of people made up in goth and metal fashions go in and out through the two-way turnstile. All of them are holding smartphones and staring at them intently as they walk in and out. As Cameron saunters closer, he pulls his cell phone out of his pocket, and we see a string of unanswered texts from him to Spencer.

Me: Spence, where are you? You're not at home. I need to talk to you. 11:12pm

Me: Ok, you're not at Chi-Pi, so you didn't go for pizza. I'll look over at the Comic Kingdom. They do that all-night table game thing tonight, right? Call me if you get this. 12:13 am

Me: Checking over at Heart of Darkness for you. Please call me if you check your messages and see this. 1:14 am

He glances at the screen and sighs, putting the phone back in his pocket. He walks toward the door and passes a young man with an elaborately coiffed mohawk sporting a prominent white stripe that runs from his scalp, up along his widow's peak and back into the mass of long hair that sweeps along the center of the young man's head. A majestic mane cascades down his shoulders. A book protrudes from the man's front pocket, and we can see the name Cioran, and the top of a title, *The Trouble...* can be made out, but the rest is obscured. The young man is on his cell phone, and as Cameron walks by, we overhear his conversation, "Humanity is just one more bifurcation on the evolutionary tree and like the dinosaurs one that has run its course. Done and dusted." he pauses listening to a reply and nodding his head in agreement with whatever he is hearing. "Our job is to accept the program and push and pull at the edifice that is known as civilization and its pathetic host, namely humanity. This is not a casual responsibility. We are literally agents of change." Cameron keeps walking, and we see the young man is leaning against the Liminal logo that was painted there on the day that Cameron last met Spencer here. He moves to the turnstile and begins to slow his pace as if he expects to be stopped, but to his surprise, the doorman unlatches the rope and motions for Cameron to go in.

Cameron nods his thanks in a rather uncertain manner and walks into the doorway, which is glowing with a faint red light, shot-through with intermittent stroboscopic flashes. We can hear strains of strange gated sounds from the Black Devil track *One To Choose*. As Cameron steps into the dark, cave like interior he stops for a minute to let his eyes adjust. He is

suddenly shoved from behind by a small group of goth-looking young

people, and we hear them murmur, almost perceptible but muddled

enough so that we are not sure what we are hearing, "Move it, geezer.

Fucking Cameron." Cameron steps aside and lets them pass, and his eyes

adjust. As his eyes adjust to the darkness, we can see more clearly, and a

DJ in a white tux is visible from across the room busily spinning the loud

music that has now become predominant. The strobe light seems to pulse

in time with the bass of the music, and Cameron moves across the dance

floor to the bar. The pulsing light causes people to appear and disappear

as he walks. As he bumps into people, we can hear a murmured series of

voices, most of the words are unclear but the name, Cameron, swims in

and out of audible perception. Cameron shakes his head a few times as if

trying to shake off the effects of the music and lights.

Suddenly, he is at the bar. The bar is garish and padded with black leather

upholstery. A glow emanates behind the bar from an unidentifiable source,

a soft, diffuse pink and blue neon-like haze. Wisps of smoke whirl along

the length of the bar. No bartender is manning the bar, nor is anyone

ordering. Cameron looks at a magazine display sitting on the bar, and he

slowly picks up a magazine that is prominently displayed there. The cover

betrays it to be the same magazine that Cameron discovered on his

doorstep, minus the lipstick additions. He puts it back in the rack somewhat hastily, jamming it back in the rack slot rather sloppily. "You wreck it you own it," a sharp female voice says, causing Cameron to jump a bit. He looks up and sees a bartender has suddenly appeared behind the bar. It is a woman, mohawked and dressed and coiffed very similarly to the young man Cameron had passed in front of the club earlier. Her facial structure is very similar to Maya's. "I didn't- I wasn't-" Camron stammers. "-Save it, That's what they all say," the bartender snarls. "You wanna fap, you gotta buy." "I- never mind," Cameron says resignedly, smoothing the pages of the magazine in the rack in a comical manner. "You buying a drink or you just gonna stand here and block other paying customers?" the bartender says with a vague New York accent. Cameron looks around, but there are no other people trying to get to the bar. "Other-" he says questioning, but before he can say more she cuts him off. "I work for the tips Romeo. No people, no tips" she nods at him as if to say 'get with the program.' Cameron tilts his head back slightly, chin forward. He looks at the bartender for a second as if in recognition but then shrugs it off. "Ok," he says pulling a crumpled twenty from his pocket, "gimme a Vesper. You can make one of those, right?" she smiles, slides his twenty off the counter and drops it somewhere out of view below the bar. "Yeah, Mr. Bond. I will have to use Lillet Blanc since they stopped making Kina Lillet, but the rest will be one hundred percent genuine," she says with an evil smile. "Wha- yeah, sure. Of course." Cameron replies somewhat uncertain. "That's what I thought," she smirks back as she begins making the drink. The music has changed now to Depeche Mode's Personal Jesus. "Question for you- I didn't get your name," Cameron says with exaggerated politeness. "That's because I didn't give it to you," she replies not looking up from her drink preparation. Cameron looks a little sheepish but continues. "When did this place change hands?" he asks. "What do you mean?" she replies. "It used to be a coffee house," he says, looking around for some evidence of the former decor. "Oh, that," she replies flatly. "That was a while ago," she says, emphasizing the word 'while.' She is shaking the drink in a martini shaker now, staring off into the distance with a look of practiced boredom. "How long?" Cameron asks, staring at the shaker with a sort of trance-like look on his face. "I dunno, man. Not my week to keep count," she says with a very lackadaisical tone. "If you had to guess?" Cameron asks, looking at her face now. She finishes shaking the drink and pours it through a strainer into a martini glass and embellishes it with a lemon rind twist. "A year or so?" she replies, pushing the drink towards him. Cameron looks off into the distance, with a glazed look in his eyes. "A- year?" he mumbles. "Eurydice" the bartender suddenly says, shaking him from his reveries. "What?" he says "My name, fappy. Eurydice. Enjoy your drink, I'm going on break." she gives him a look of half pity and half disgust and then withdraws to a room behind the bar. Cameron stands, staring at his drink. He pulls his phone out of his pocket and thumbs the screen to life. We see that Spencer has finally answered his last text.

Spencer: I am here. I'm over by the DJ. Where are you?

Cameron looks towards the DJ just in time to see Spencer going through a curtain that is hanging over a doorway, and we get a quick glimpse of a hallway, before the curtain swings downward, blocking the view. Cameron lifts his phone and texts back:

Me: I'm here too. I'm by the bar, but I just saw you by the DJ. I'll come to you.

He begins walking across the dance floor, leaving his drink behind. He is navigating around the goth and metal bedecked denizens bopping to the music. Everyone on the dance floor seems to be staring at smartphones being held at eye level. Cameron bumps his way through the crowd, and we can hear the name Cameron being whispered in the background, possibly in the music or possibly from the phone dancers. The source of the whispering is not clear, but it is clear that Cameron can hear it, as he twists his head around looking for the source, in vain. He finally emerges from the crowd and makes a beeline for the curtain. He darts behind the DJ and lifts the curtain. As he does, the DJ turns and says, "He took a face from the ancient gallery..." and then turns back around to the DJ station. Cameron looks back at what lies behind the curtain, and we see a long hall with multiple doors, some made of heavy wood, ala medieval style and others which appear to be barred cell doors. The walls are covered in textured, red patterned Victorian wallpaper, with low red-tinged light coming from ornate ceiling lamps. Cameron moves under the curtain completely and allows it to fall limply behind him.

The music is muted now, a lot more than may be expected from a mere curtain. He moves further down the hall, gingerly, looking around cautiously. "Spencer?" he calls out, his voice cracking. He stops and clears his throat. "Spence?" Cameron is now in front of one of the cell doors, and we can see that the room inside is decked out with BDSM gear, like a leather padded T cross and various whips and chains hanging from racks. He continues to walk further down the hall. Suddenly his phone buzzes, and he clumsily claws it free from his pocket and looks at the screen. He sees Spencer has responded.

Spencer: Awesome. I can't believe you're here. Never thought this was your kind of place. I'm in room 64. Just ask the DJ, and he'll point you in the right direction.

Cameron looks up at a wooden door that he has stopped in front of and sees the number 23 on it. He walks further down the hall, passing more cell doors and wooden doors interspersed. He passes one door that has a Liminal logo carved on it as if it was deeply etched with a large knife. He doesn't notice the carved door, but he then arrives at a door with the number 64 on it caddy-cornered from the carved door. He hesitates but then finally knocks. "Spence?" he calls out. "It's me." The door opens from the inside, and Spencer is standing there smiling. Behind him, we can see a large fancy articulated gamer chair that is facing a giant tv screen displaying a first-person shooter game on pause.

The rest of the room looks like some sort of gamer's idea of utopia. Snack machines, giant speakers, shelves full of various types of controllers, gun, and driving game accessories, VR goggles, gloves, and assorted unidentifiable gamer gear is stacked neatly in rows on shelves that line the room. Spencer motions Cameron inside. "C'mon. Mi casa es su casa!" he says smiling. "So glad you decided to join us here in the land of the living." "What is this place?" Cameron asks looking around. "What happened to the coffee..." Spencer cuts him off, "Man, you really do need to get out more," he grins, "this hasn't been the coffee clutch depot for some time now." He moves over to the game console and flips a switch and the giant screen switches from the paused game to the Electric Sheep screensaver.

"Spencer, I- Maya left, things have gotten out of control, I'm not sure what's going on anymore-" Cameron gushes. "Shit man. Ok. Shit. Maya left?" he says, with a tone of concern. "Yeah, I- I fucked up. I- I don't know what the fuck is going on anymore. I walk through life, and it seems like a fucking Fellini film, and I just seem to take it all in like it's mostly normal..." "Buddy," Spencer cuts in, "Look, I have this room rented for another 3 hours. We can hang, talk it out. I even have beer." He walks over to a market-style reach-in glass cooler full of beer. He pulls out two cans of some sort of microbrew that has a very prominent picture of a black cat with its back arched. He hands one to Cameron, who takes it, pops the top and chugs down half of it in one long draw. "Now, tell me what the fuck is going on," Spencer says. "Spence, I have a weird question to ask you," Cameron says, and then he takes another long draw of beer. "Sure man, anything." Spencer has a look of genuine concern in his eyes. "What- is- my name?" Cameron asks, emphasizing each word, as we see what looks like the muted glow of a yellow circuit board pattern pulsing beneath the skin of Spencer's face. There is a long pause as Spencer searches Cameron' s face and then he looks down and sighs. "Aw, man. I think I've been here before," he says, gently. "Spencer," Cameron says very emphatically, "What- is- my- name?" Spencer looks at him with a pained look on his face, and he opens his mouth to speak, but before he can, his head explodes, showering Cameron's face in brain bits and gore. Cameron opens his mouth and makes a "puh" sound like the sound one makes when surfacing from a long immersion in water. His eyes dart over to a wisp of smoke emanating from a hole in the wall just to the left of the giant screen on the wall. Spencer's mostly headless body slumps over onto Cameron, who holds the body up at first but then, with a look of horror on his face, he lets Spencer's lifeless body slump to the floor. His mouth is open, but no sound comes out, except a faint high-pitched wheeze of sorts. He stands looking down at Spencer, and then he sees something move past the hole where the smoke was formerly coming out, just a glimpse of movement, and he turns and begins to run. He runs out the door, down the hall and darts from behind the curtain.

As soon as he emerges from behind the curtain, the music comes back blasting at full volume, StaticX, *Wisconsin Death Trip*. Cameron looks up at the dance floor, and everyone is holding their cell phone up and staring at him as if they are all videoing the moment. He turns and runs toward an exit door, with the emergency bar type release. As he makes his way toward the door, he gets his legs tangled up in the base of a large 5-foot tall candelabra, causing it to teeter back and forth, which snuffs out one of the seven burning candles atop it. The candelabra finally tips all the way over and catches a camouflage-patterned drape on fire as we hear the voice of William Burroughs over the club's speakers say, " first to leave at the moment of death, is Ren... This corresponds to my Director" Cameron stumbles forward, arms outstretched and finally reaches the door bursting through it, out into a vacant alley. He bends over and vomits behind a dumpster, with a large spray-painted Liminal logo behind him. He looks around wildly and then begins running down the alley. Smoke pours from the door he exited, and a fire alarm goes off as he fades into the night.

TOTAL MELTDOWN

We see Cameron walking down a series of dark streets now, from the look of it, he's back in the neighborhood where he chased the burglar earlier in the day. His clothes are disheveled and very dirty. HIs face is also dirty and tracks of exposed skin record recent rivulets of tears that have etched marks on the facial dirt. His shirt has vomit stains and dirt on it in various places, and his pants are dirty and ripped in several spots. He staggers into an abandoned building, making sure that no one is following him, and walks up the stairs to the roof. The fire-door locks behind him as he steps onto the roof. He stops, looks at the door, pulling on it and then resigned he repeats to himself, "The only way out is through" as he walks across the roof to the ledge. He looks over the edge for a while and then eventually, he sits down with his legs dangling over the edge. He pulls a wadded napkin out of his pocket and then fishes a short pencil stub from his slightly ripped and drooping shirt pocket. He swings his legs back and forth while he busily scribbles on the napkin. Without looking up, he says aloud, "You left me when I needed you most Maya." he then looks up, and we see Maya sitting on the building's air conditioning unit. "Wrong, Cameron. You left me long ago," she says. "Why do you call me that?" he asks, still not looking at her. "Because that's your name. Always has been. But I guess when you checked out last year, you left that name behind?" she asks. "I don't recall-" he begins then stops. "If Cameron isn't your name, then what is? I told you my name." Cameron looks up, and now Eurydice is sitting where Maya once sat. We can see that the two are almost identical except for the hair, style of dress and the facial expression. Eurydice has what is called "resting bitch face," whereas Maya's natural expression is much softer. Cameron doesn't seem to be fazed by the switch, and he looks at Eurydice wistfully before finally answering, "I don't remember," he finally answers. He then looks away and goes back to his scribbling. "You left me a year ago," Maya/Eurydice continues, "and then you had another chance to rescue me, but you left me again in Hades." "You mean, the Heart of Darkness?" he answers, still not looking at her. "Yes," she answers "you left again, you left all of us." He looks up, and now he sees Spencer sitting on the A/C unit, the front of his shirt covered in blood and gore and his head being held together but what appears to be bloody duct tape. "You left us all buddy. You left us a year ago, and you just left us again, in hell. Some hero you turned out to be." Spencer says, with a smirk. "This thing is bigger than you, bigger than me, bigger than all of us. It is literally rewriting reality and reprogramming the collective unconscious. Basically, you have unleashed a virus that is rewriting the lowest level of reality comprehension for god knows what purpose. Maybe no purpose at all maybe some purpose that only makes sense to it but that is beyond our comprehension. One thing is certain, it has bored a hole right straight from the liminal realm to this causal reality, and nothing is ever going to be the same." he tosses his head and snorts after he says this as if he just got the punchline to a joke he had been pondering. Cameron stops scribbling and lays the note down behind him. He then takes off his wristwatch and lays it on the napkin like a paperweight. He then slides his wallet and cell phone out of their respective pockets and lays them gently next to the napkin and watch. "If I didn't know better, I'd say you were about to kill yourself," Spencer says, in an almost jovial tone. "You're not here." Cameron says, looking at him for a few seconds, "but I wish you were," he adds glumly.

Cameron stands up and then looks at the A/C unit, and Spencer is gone. "The only way out is-" He looks down to a precipitous drop. With arms akimbo, he looks up at the rising sun and steps off the ledge. He we see him falling slowly and then after a long slow-motion sequence of him tumbling end over end with a serene look on is his face, we return to real-time, and he lands with a thud on an adjacent rooftop. "-through" he finishes the sentence as he lands. He is lying on his back looking stunned. We see an old flip-style cell phone lying next to him on the tarpaper rooftop.

The phone suddenly starts ringing. He slowly picks it up and answers. We can hear the 911 operator's voice on the line, his tone now pleasant and melodious. The operator begins by saying, "Condolences and Congratulations" to which Cameron replies in an unsure tone, "Uh, thanks?" "Look, Cameron, we weren't sure about you at first. I mean, you did find the semantic code and release it into the wild, but by all accounts, you were ignorant of what you were doing- on a conscious level at least. I mean, there are no accidents, not really, right?" you can hear the glee in the operator's voice. Cameron is still listening with a quizzical look on his face. "I was always rooting for you. Some people here…" "Where's here?" Cameron interrupts, "Oh, here, you know, at the headquarters of the Liminal Group" the operator replies, "The- Liminal- Group-," Cameron says, pausing after each word, "the group I invented for my game?" he adds, "No, well yes, ok, yes and no. I'd explain in detail but it's liminal so we can't approach it head-on, only sideways. It's as simple and as complicated as an intel organization seeding disinformation, that come back and later unknowingly consuming that very disinformation which then transforms it into information that is then actionable." he says. Cameron is still listening and has a puzzled look on his face. "It will more or less make sense in time, more or less. You already get it on an instinctual level or you would not still be here," he says in a sing-song voice. "I just tried to kill myself," Cameron replies. "Not really, not really or you'd be dead. You knew on some level that you'd hit that rooftop…" "No, I didn't see it, I really meant to die…" Cameron interrupted, "Yes, that's why it was successful as a ritual, but unconsciously, it was simply symbolic…" "I am getting sick of this bullshit!" Cameron explodes, interrupting. "Ok, Cameron- your real name, now if not always-" he adds parenthetically, "you are free to be whoever you want to be. Be Cameron, take up a cause, don't take up a cause, because you have earned your walking papers mister and we always reward a good deed. You set us free so now we set you free. You have the

ability now to surf the reality changes that are coming. You have the evolutionary advantage. What you choose to do with that is up to you." operator man says. "What if I choose to end you?" Cameron says slowly and with deliberation. "Well within the bounds of possibilities and even within the realm of expected probabilities, but still a free choice and still yours to make. Opposition is actually not a bad thing. It gives each side the tension and dynamics needed to grow something new." We can hear something scratching against the receiver and then a click as the operator closes the line. Cameron looks at the phone for a few seconds as we see it is covered in streaks of fresh blood, and then suddenly, he throws the phone off the building and walks to the ledge. He fiddles with something that seems to be stuck in his right ear. We see a little sliver of shiny metal that he starts pulling on. Slowly, what looks like a recurved paperclip or fishing hook with tiny notches on it slides out from under the skin around his ear. Walking toward the fire door, he sees a small hole above its keyless handle, and he slots the metal shard into it. The door opens.
Fade to black

It's daytime, and we are in a cafe. We see, Cameron, looking very cleaned up compared to the last time we saw him. His clothes are clean and pressed, and he looks rested. He is sitting at a table, eating a traditional American breakfast, and reading a newspaper. We zoom in on an article that says a man named Cameron (last name obscured by Cameron's thumb holding the paper) died after leaping from a mid-city building that was in the process of demolition. He has no next of kin, and no note was found to indicate a motive. Cameron pulls out a twenty dollar bill and lays it on top of the check as he stands to leave. We see a slight smile on his face.

Fade to black

We are looking over the shoulder of an unidentified person as they are checking email/Readdlt forums - emails/Readdits are all about strange occurrences regarding the disappearance of the creator of "Liminal" the Living Book/Game. The text is rife with conspiratorial musings that he was "Onto something bigger" and he was silenced by "the powers that be." We then see the computer being shut down.

Fade to black

We see an unidentified bearded man, wearing a green hoodie and aviator glasses, which we glimpse momentarily as he turns away from what he is doing. As we pull back, we see that the man has spray painted a large red circle and slash over a Liminal logo that is painted on a wall. He examines his handiwork for a second and then crosses the street. He then paints Liminal logo on the wall directly across the street from the one he just crossed out. He does not cross this one out with the red circle/slash. He then turns to admire his handiwork, and we see that this is Cameron. We see a messenger bag hanging across his shoulders with the bag itself slung across his buttocks. Protruding from the bag is a sheaf of papers, and we zoom in to see the typed words across the top of the top sheet-

"Liminal- A Screenplay by Cameron," with the last name hidden in the folds of the bag. Cameron smiles as he puts the spray can into a messenger bag and walks away into the dark city night.